# HORIZON
## THE GAME

A small group of survivors steps from
the wreckage of a plane . . .
**And you're one of them.**

## JOIN THE RACE FOR SURVIVAL!

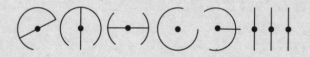

1. Download the app or go to **scholastic.com/horizon**
2. Log in to create your character.
3. Go to the Sequencer in your home camp.
4. Input the above musical sequence.
5. Claim your prize!

**Available for tablet, phone, and browser.**
**scholastic.com/horizon**

# HORIZON

## DEADZONE

## JENNIFER A. NIELSEN

SCHOLASTIC INC.

This book is a work of fiction. Names, characters, places, and incidents are either the product of the author's imagination or are used fictitiously, and any resemblance to actual persons, living or dead, business establishments, events, or locales is entirely coincidental.

ISBN 978-1-338-12144-5

10 9 8 7 6 5 4 3 2 1    18 19 20 21 22

Printed in the U.S.A.    40
This edition first printing 2018

Book design by Abby Dening

*To those who battle against the odds;*
*may victory be yours*

# PRESS RELEASE FOR INCIDENT INVOLVING AERO HORIZON FLIGHT 16

THE FOLLOWING IS THE MOST CURRENT INFORMATION AVAILABLE.

Aero Horizon Flight 16, bound for Tokyo, Japan, recorded normal takeoff.

- - - - - - - - - - - - - - - - - - - - - - - - - - - - - - - - - - - - -

The aircraft received a mild weather warning as it passed near Fairbanks, Alaska. Approximately two minutes later, a bird strike triggered emergency alarms.

- - - - - - - - - - - - - - - - - - - - - - - - - - - - - - - - - - - - -

Final cockpit recordings suggest massive structural damage. The aircraft is presumed to have been lost in the arctic region. No traces of the craft have been found.

- - - - - - - - - - - - - - - - - - - - - - - - - - - - - - - - - - - - -

All 497 passengers and 16 cabin crew are presumed dead.

- - - - - - - - - - - - - - - - - - - - - - - - - - - - - - - - - - - - -

# Molly

I n the end, saving them would be up to her.

Molly knew this in the same way she knew her own name, or the way she knew that the sun would rise each day, just as it had this morning.

Actually, the sun wasn't a problem. It was the moon, or *moons*, that worried her. Wherever they were now, whatever this place was, images of two moons were somehow projected into the atmosphere. One was red, the other was green, and those moons—alien, unfathomable, and cold—symbolized everything that was wrong with this place. Molly couldn't shake the feeling that the moons *meant* something, something important to their survival.

Seven of them remained, out of over five hundred on a plane bound for Tokyo. After being ripped apart like an aluminum can, their plane had crashed four days ago. Was it really only four days?

"Four days!" Javi groaned, as if reading her thoughts. He was one of Molly's best friends, and certainly her best friend among the survivors. "Four days since I've eaten a real meal! I'd eat my shoelaces if I still had some Tabasco sauce to dip them in."

"Shoelaces have no nutritional value," Anna said. "You'd do better eating the dirt." Anna was . . . extremely honest. Too honest, sometimes.

"If I'm this hungry on day five, I might just try it." Javi turned back to Oliver. "I dreamed about Tabasco sauce last night. We fed it to a dreadful duck of doom—the same one that slashed Molly. Smoke came out of its beak."

Oliver smiled, but not really. Molly was worried about him. He was the smallest and youngest, and had an innocence about him that was being leeched away by the reality of their situation. At least Javi was distracting him with what remained of the robot they'd salvaged from the crash.

"It made it through a plane crash; it could've won that soccer game!" Oliver said proudly.

Molly rolled her eyes. What did a soccer-playing robot matter now? She, Javi, Anna, and Oliver were all that remained of their Killbot robotics team. Today would have been the final round of competition at the Robot Soccer World Championship.

For months, getting to that championship had been top priority. Now her biggest goal—her only goal—was to stay alive. Plane crashes into impossibly strange environments had a funny way of changing one's perspective.

There were three other survivors with them, including two sisters, Kira and Akiko. They spoke fluent Japanese and French, but only a few words of English. The final member of the group was Yoshi, who was half-American and half-Japanese and carried a chip on his shoulder roughly the size of Manhattan.

Molly looked around. "Has anyone seen Yoshi yet?"

The only answer she got was a shrug from Anna, who was standing behind Javi and Oliver, watching them work. Didn't anyone else feel the same urgency to break camp? They'd never escape this place if they didn't keep moving.

Molly tossed an empty backpack at Kira, motioning that she should begin filling it. But Kira only bent back over her drawing, blocking Molly from view with a curtain of hair, which was black except for a streak of purple. Kira came across as tough and a little angry, her body tense as if always ready for a fight. She was also an amazing artist who was currently working on a picture of her sister. Because nothing said "we're fighting for our lives" like pencil sketches.

Akiko was very different from Kira. She was the shy one, who more often than not looked like she'd prefer to fade into the background. She came alive when she played her flute, though.

Even now, when the purpose of her playing was to lure in a slide-whistle bird for their last meal before the group broke camp.

"Enough!" Molly announced. "Everyone get up and help me pack! We need to get moving." Her eyes settled on Akiko. "Bird or no bird."

Akiko lowered her flute. "Bird," she repeated.

"We should stay here long enough to find more food," Anna said. "We burned through a lot of our supplies in the jungle."

*Literally burned through them*, thought Molly. They'd experimented with the settings on one of the two strange devices they'd found. It had sparked the broken plane back to life, lighting up its technology so much that it exploded, nearly taking them with it.

Oliver turned his hopeful puppy-dog eyes in the direction Yoshi had gone earlier that morning. "Yoshi went hunting. He'll find more food."

"Unless I failed." Everyone turned to see Yoshi stomp into camp from the opposite direction, his sword in its sheath at his side. Molly had pieced enough together to know that the sword was very old and very valuable.

*"Tabemono ga nai?"* Kira asked.

"No, there isn't any food, and I don't want to hear any complaints," Yoshi said with a scowl. "We'll just have to make do with what we have."

Kira apparently understood his tone if not his words. Molly felt the group's mood sink, which was the last thing they needed. She forced a smile to her face. "Okay, then let's take inventory. If you have anything of value—and I mean, if you have even a stick of gum in your pocket that you've been saving for later—then bring it forward!"

Nobody had a stick of gum, apparently, or maybe they just weren't about to sacrifice their one chance at a minty fresh mouth to someone else. But other items did come forward.

Anna brought out the two devices they had found in the jungle. These were metal disks in the shape of a donut and about the size of a CD. Each had rotating inner and outer rings, with unfamiliar symbols on both rings. When they aligned, the matching symbols lit up, and pressing those lit symbols made things happen. Crazy things that would've turned Isaac Newton's world upside down, perhaps literally. With a twist of the rings, gravity got lighter or heavier, technology went to zero or powered up. Molly suspected one setting affected the temperature in the area—something was holding back the arctic ice, after all—but she wasn't interested in testing that theory if it risked sending the rift into a sudden ice age.

"What else do we have?" Molly asked.

They had a battery taken from a cave-dwelling robot Anna had smashed, two backpacks, a canteen half-full of water, a handful of flares, some packaged food, some bungee cords, and a radio that played only static.

"It's not enough." Everyone turned to look at Yoshi firmly

shaking his head. "If you'd seen what I have, seen what's ahead . . ."

Javi's brows pressed together. "What'd you see?"

"Nothing but desert. As far as the eye can see, there's nothing but dry clay soil and bare rock and sand. No food. No water." He turned to Molly. "No hope of rescue."

Molly wasn't going to let the others know how his words left knots in her stomach and sweat on her palms. Instead, she made sure they saw her smile and shrug Yoshi's warning away. "We'll rescue ourselves, then."

"How?" Oliver's eyes widened. "We don't have enough stuff to survive a backyard campout. How do we survive a desert?"

"We wasted too many supplies already," Yoshi said. "You guys were using flares like they grew on trees."

"Or like they protected us from what flew out of the trees!" Javi said. "We had to use them to keep the shredder birds from ripping us apart."

"At least in the jungle we were able to find water and food and shelter," Anna said. "We won't be so lucky in the desert. If there's no water, then there are no plants or animals. No trees for shelter."

"Or wood to build a fire," Yoshi added. "So even if we catch a bird, there'll be no way to cook it."

Oliver moaned. "We're goners for sure. Let's just stay here."

"There's no choice but to go forward," Javi argued. "If the map Anna saw is right, there's some kind of man-made structure out there at the far end of the rift. A building means people, answers . . ."

Yoshi scoffed. "What if we don't like those answers?"

"Molly might *need* the answers," Javi countered. "Maybe someone there can tell us what's wrong with her shoulder and—"

"My shoulder is fine," Molly said. That wasn't quite true. The injury to her shoulder from the dreadful duck of doom was far more serious than the bird's name implied, with a green rash slowly spreading across her skin. It didn't hurt, but it wasn't healing, either. Not that she would tell anyone how bad it looked. They had larger problems. She planned to keep it covered and to keep her mouth shut about it.

"Maybe we should wait one more day," Anna said.

"Or another week," Yoshi added.

Javi stood on a rock where everyone could see him. "Stop it, all of you! We can't stay here and we shouldn't waste time hoping a rescue will come, because it probably won't. Our only choice is to cross the rift and find out what's in that building. Let's stop saying we *can't* and figure out how we *can*!"

The group looked from him over to Molly. She took a deep breath, then said, "Javi's right. We are smart enough to figure this out, no matter how bad it seems. We can do this. We just have to work together."

"That's fine for your Killbot team," Yoshi said. "You know each other and take care of each other. What about me and the sisters?"

Akiko and Kira smiled, as if they knew he was talking about them.

"From now on, we're all on Team Killbot." Molly made sure she looked each person in the eye as she spoke. "All of us."

She thought Yoshi looked especially pleased by that, though she wasn't sure why. She had been careful not to treat him or the sisters as outsiders. Now she wondered if Yoshi had simply never been part of a team before. He seemed like the kind of kid who had trouble fitting in.

So he wasn't a loner entirely by choice. That would be good to keep in mind if she was going to keep everyone moving in the same direction.

Molly continued, "And if we're going to be a single team, then we're going to function like one. To start, we need a leader." She looked around the group. "Any volunteers?"

Javi laughed. "Right. Everyone who votes for Molly, raise your hand." He was the first to do so, but the rest of the team immediately followed, even Yoshi, who might have had other ideas, and Kira and Akiko, who had no way of knowing what they'd just voted for.

Molly hesitated, instantly feeling the weight of leadership. She finally said, "All right, but I can't do it alone. Everyone gets a responsibility."

No one spoke. Except for Akiko, who said, "Bird," for some reason.

Molly looked around the group. "Javi, you're my second-in-command."

His face lit up. "Like the vice president? Deputy?"

"Annoying sidekick," Anna said.

"First Officer Spock," Yoshi added. "Can we call you Spock?"

"I'll work on my own title," Javi said.

Molly turned to Yoshi. "You'll be in charge of defending us. Kira and Akiko can look for food. I want Anna to specifically find us water while we're out there."

"What about me?" Oliver said.

Molly wished she could roll him in Bubble Wrap until he was safely home, but she knew he needed a job, to feel as much a part of the team as everyone else.

"You're our lookout," she finally said. "If something is coming, I want you to be the first to warn us."

Oliver smiled and nodded enthusiastically.

"Bird," Akiko repeated.

This time they looked in the direction she was pointing her chin. A slide-whistle bird had landed right in their camp. Yoshi stepped forward with his sword raised.

"All right," Molly said a moment later. "Let's eat, and then we move forward."

## Yoshi

Yoshi had tried to warn the others. He'd told them how big the desert was, how empty, but that didn't stop their jaws from falling open when seeing it firsthand. They stood on the edge of a rocky overlook, the jungle at their backs and a wide, barren valley before them.

"I'll bet this is what forever looks like," Javi said, shaking his head like he couldn't accept the scale of what they'd have to cross. Yoshi wondered if he'd give that same "go Team Killbot" speech now that he'd seen this place for himself.

"Where's all the green?" Oliver asked.

A few miserable-looking plants were scattered across patches of hardened clay soil, but they hardly qualified as green. Maybe "bread-mold green." Or "how-did-you-vomit-up-that-color green?" These plants wouldn't be edible, or provide shade, and probably didn't need much water to survive, so there was no point in digging beneath them.

Molly walked up beside Yoshi, folding her arms in determination. "You were right. This will be an . . . interesting challenge. How do we even get down there? This hill we're on is very steep."

"We could switch on low gravity," Anna suggested.

Javi frowned. "And push off a cactus into the air? No, thank you!"

Several possible trails stretched out ahead of them, each one a perilous choose-your-own-adventure through an uneven maze of boulders, crevices, and patches of spiny cacti. Gusts of hot wind raced up the slope from the desert floor, unpredictable and at times strong enough that Akiko had already taken her sister's hand for balance. Complicating what was already going to be a difficult descent, a river ran down the slope as well. It wasn't a river of water, naturally, because nothing here was that simple. This river was thick and slow, like spilled syrup, and it glowed with a green color similar to Molly's shoulder. Yoshi wasn't going anywhere near it.

"We'll never get across all of this," Akiko whispered to him.

"Even if we fly," Kira added.

Then the girls said something to each other in French, which was particularly annoying. He was the only other Killbot who could understand Japanese, so when they switched to French, it meant they were deliberately excluding him. Maybe he'd quit translating between English and Japanese for a while, let them remember what it felt like to be left out of a conversation. He was tired of translating anyway.

"We'll never cross it by standing here," Molly said, leading the way down a trail that Yoshi figured was as good as any other. They walked single file, with him taking up the rear, one hand on his sword. Just in case.

Everyone walked in total silence, until Javi began whistling. It happened to be a song Yoshi had heard once as a child. The tune had come on the radio while he was in the car with his father, who had cracked a rare smile and turned the volume up. The memory caught him completely off guard.

What was his father thinking about now, four days after Yoshi's plane had vanished? Was he worried? Was he sad? Did he have any regrets? Because Yoshi sure did—mostly regrets about getting on that plane in the first place.

Javi whistled louder now, each note burrowing deeper into Yoshi's nerves. Before long, Akiko joined in, her whistle sounding like an echo of her flute. Then Oliver began whistling, though he wasn't even close to the correct pitch. He was so far off that he seemed to be whistling another song altogether.

Molly suddenly raised one hand and the whistling stopped. She turned back to them. "Sorry, guys, I led us to a dead end. There's a bunch of huge rocks ahead."

Yoshi motioned to the right. "This way." Everyone followed him now to a different trail. Javi pursed his lips, and Yoshi shook his head. "This is a 'no whistling' trail. My trail, my rules."

"Your trail is slime-covered." Javi grinned as he pointed farther down the path to where the green goo created a ditch too wide to safely jump. "I'll take us to a new trail. A trail where whistling is mandatory."

Yoshi rolled his eyes, strongly considering taking any other route down the hill. But he was supposed to protect his team, whistling or not, so he had to follow them.

Molly waited for Yoshi, then walked along beside him at the rear of their group. "Does it feel like we're being steered? Like someone is blocking some of these paths on purpose?"

Yoshi shrugged. "If so, it's wasted effort. One way or another, we'll reach the bottom." But he tightened his grip on the hilt of his sword.

"Look. Trees!" Anna said. She stepped forward and pointed off to the right. There was only one tree of any size, really, surrounded by a few sad bushes that couldn't even be bothered to produce leaves, but she seemed encouraged. "There'll be water below them," she said. "I think we should go in that direction."

Molly sighed, switching her gaze between the one sign of life in the desert and the path they'd been walking. She turned to Javi. "What do you think, deputy?"

Javi shoved his hands into his pockets, or what remained of his pockets after the shredder birds had finished with him back in the jungle. "I think if there's one tree here, then there'll be others. We should keep going the most direct path, because of . . . because it's fastest."

Javi cast a not-so-furtive glance at Molly's injury. Yoshi looked again, too. She kept it covered, but her wound was far more serious than anything a bandage and a couple of aspirin could fix.

Molly nodded back at Javi. "I agree. Our target is the building. We can't get distracted."

"Even for water?" Oliver asked.

"We'll find more," Molly told him. "Besides, I'm tired of dead ends. We're going to fly. Maybe we'll cross this whole desert in only a few hours."

Somehow, Yoshi doubted that. Whoever built this place, ease of travel had clearly not been their top priority.

So who did build this place, and why? And why had nobody ever found it? You'd think that with all the satellites and airplanes crisscrossing the globe every day, maybe someone would have looked at a giant rift in the arctic and said, "Hey, that's not normal!"

On Molly's orders, everyone else had begun connecting themselves to the bungee cords to start their flight over the desert. She handed Yoshi one end of a cord. "Put Akiko and Kira next to you, since you can speak with them, and Anna can go on the end to work the device for your group."

Akiko and Kira were still speaking in French. Yoshi told them in Japanese that if they didn't cut it out, he and Anna were going to leave them behind.

"You're not our boss," Kira said, swiping the end of the bungee cord from him. "If we knew English, we'd speak it."

Yoshi scowled. "Then learn it."

"Maybe we will," Akiko said, though her eyes were lowered, as if she were hoping to avoid any further argument.

Yoshi preferred that, too. The sisters didn't deserve his irritation. He was just anxious about what lay ahead, and aside from the sisters, everyone had become far too quiet.

"Only when it is silent can you hear the whispers of the universe," his father used to say, something that had never made sense to Yoshi until now. The desert air felt brittle with silence. And if the universe was whispering anything to him in the eerie quiet, it was a single word:

*Run.*

# 3

## Javi

Javi's experience jumping in low gravity was mixed, at best. Nothing in his history beat the thrill of leaping into the air and feeling his body float upward, then slowly drift back to earth. Or . . . drift across the rift. Hey, it rhymed! He'd have to start using that line.

However, low gravity had also introduced him to shredder birds, feathered little demons that had done to his clothes and arms exactly what their name implied. He hoped the birds had been left behind in the jungle. No trees to perch on, no birds, right?

Javi had a bungee cord tied around his waist, connecting him to Molly and Oliver, with Molly controlling the device for their group. On her cue, they all pushed off the ground, immediately stretching their bodies straight, hoping it would create an arrow effect into the air.

They wouldn't get as high here as they had in the jungle, where the trees gave them a canopy to bounce off. But as long as they got higher than the boulders and the cacti, and they stayed clear of whatever that gooey green river was, Javi figured they'd be fine.

Oliver shouted over to Javi, "What's the mathematical formula to calculate friction's drag on an object in motion?"

Javi twisted around to Molly. "Do you know the answer?"

She looked up from the device. "No, but I bet we can work it out."

"I guess we start by figuring out what causes the friction," Javi said.

"Exactly!" Oliver pushed his hands through the air, as if swimming closer to Javi. "Does the desert floor create friction against my foot as I walk? Or does the weight of my foot create friction against the desert floor?"

On the other bungee cord nearby, Yoshi groaned. "Could you guys talk about anything else? I'm falling asleep over here!"

Akiko said Yoshi's name, then pointed to Oliver and said something in Japanese. Yoshi responded, "Pizza," then added something more in Japanese.

"What was she asking?" Javi asked. Pizza sounded pretty great to him right now.

Yoshi smiled. "She wanted in on your conversation but that was too boring to translate. So I told her you were debating if the rift offers any pizza delivery."

Javi started to laugh, but now he was asking himself the very same question. Obviously there wasn't *delivery*, but he wondered if there could be pizza at the building at the end of the rift.

Pizza. Thick crust piled high with sausage, cheese, and jalapeños. His mouth watered. Just the thought of it made him eager to hurry to that building. For Molly, of course. But maybe for pizza, too. They were making good progress down the slope.

A sharp gust of wind that swept up from the desert floor ended that idea. It smacked Javi across the chest and the rest of Team Killbot as well, pushing them far too high in the air. Wind rushed past his ears.

"I see more trees!" Anna cried.

"What?" Molly was at the far end of the bungee cord, higher than the rest of them. "We can't hear you!"

Anna cupped her hand around her ear. "We can't steer to you, either. I said those are big trees!"

"Yes, it's a big breeze!" Molly looked over at Javi as if Anna had just stated the obvious. He only chuckled to himself.

A second gust of wind separated the two groups, carrying Yoshi's group higher on the slope and pushing Javi's toward the desert floor.

"We need to stay together!" Molly shouted over to Anna. "Turn on the gravity!"

Anna shook her head, indicating she hadn't heard anything, and Molly pointed down to the ground.

"We're too high!" Javi yelled at Molly. "If you drop us from here, it's Caleb all over again."

He shouldn't have said that, shouldn't have reminded Molly and Oliver and anyone else who'd heard. Caleb had survived the plane crash, but had then discovered the device's heavy gravity setting, paying for it with his life.

"I'll do it gradually," Molly said. "Hopefully the others will see what we're doing and come down near us. We'll make another jump after the wind dies down."

*Dies down?* Javi groaned. Did she have to phrase it that way?

But her idea seemed to be working. He felt an increasing tug in his gut pulling him downward, then the queasiness that came with floating. Then they were heavy again. Molly was turning the device on and off, lowering them a bit at a time. At this rate, it might be a hard landing, but not so hard as to break bones.

He looked around for Yoshi's group, but they were already below the ridgeline. He heard them shouting at one another, but in the wind, couldn't tell exactly where they were.

"Javi, watch out!" Oliver said.

A final gust of wind had pulled them sideways and now, only a few feet from the ground, Javi was directly over a patch of cacti. Spiny, thorny, prickly cacti that seemed to widen their stems to greet him.

"I knew it," he muttered. "I knew this would happen, just knew it."

Inches from landing, his gut twisted again and he floated a few seconds longer, just enough for the wind to carry him past the cacti patch. He looked up at Molly who was landing a few feet away, smiling as she shut off their device.

"You're welcome," she said.

Javi brushed a hand through his hair as he bumped to the ground, and looked back at what he'd just escaped. His respect for Molly, as a leader and as a friend, had just increased sharply. He smiled at the pun.

They untied themselves from the bungee cord, and while Molly collected it into her backpack, she said, "Let's spread out and see if anyone can spot the rest of our group below."

Javi went to the right, toward the trees Anna had pointed out when they were in the air. If he could climb to the top of one, he'd have a much better view. Molly and Oliver went in the opposite direction, the way they'd last seen Yoshi's group drift in the wind.

"Be careful, Javi!" Molly called at his back as he wandered out of her sight.

"Javi!" No, *that* was Molly's voice, there, ahead in the trees. How did she get over there?

"Mol?" He hurried closer to the trees.

"Javi! Be careful, Javi!" she called again.

"Why? What's wrong?"

These trees weren't anything like the massive, powerful specimens they'd seen in the jungle. These were mostly gnarled, knotty branches with tufts of green spines at the ends. The branches would be easy enough to climb, but chances were high he'd come down with needles in his backside.

"Javi!"

Javi turned in a circle, looking for Molly. If she were here, he'd have seen her.

"Careful, Javi, careful!"

Javi finally located the source of the sound; it was coming from a small, bright green bird at the top of one tree. A mockingbird, except the ones back at home could only imitate the tweeting of other birds. This one had heard Molly's voice and imitated it perfectly.

"Aren't you cute?" Javi reached for the lower limbs of the tree and as he did, more of the birds flocked into the branches. A few at first, then ten, then dozens.

"Careful, Javi! Careful, Javi!" Every bird was saying it now, a chorus of Molly voices singing to him. This was so weird, and so cool. But mostly weird.

He climbed up to a higher branch and now the birds surrounded him.

"How do I go home?" he asked the birds.

Their voices shifted, replicating his own. "Go home. Go home, Javi!"

Javi stretched out his hand, wondering if one of the birds might trust him enough to come along for a little walk. The others would love to see this!

"It's okay," he whispered. "I won't hurt you."

"Hurt you," the birds repeated. "Hurt you."

And the one nearest to his hand bit it. An actual bite that drew blood. The other birds followed, swarming at him and biting wherever they found flesh. Javi yelled and waved his arms at them, and they yelled in his same voice and waved their wings back.

He thrashed around enough to make them fly away, but lost his balance and fell backward onto the ground. The impact was so shocking that it took him a moment to feel the cacti needles in his rear end.

Served him right for trusting a bird that had been telling him, "Careful, Javi."

Somewhere in the distance, he heard Molly calling his name. Even as he closed his eyes, he was unsure if it was her, or if the birds were coming back to peck at him again.

# 4

## Anna

Anna's group touched down at the bottom of the steep hill. Everyone untied themselves from the bungee cord and started to look for Molly's group, who were probably farther uphill. But where? The gust of wind had taken them higher and out of sight, making it impossible to track them.

Kira and Yoshi were arguing in Japanese, and Kira kept motioning up the hill. Finally, she seemed to give up. She grabbed Akiko's hand, pulled her off to the side, and began speaking to her in French. Yoshi turned his back on them all, scowling out across the desert floor.

Anna didn't understand why they were so upset.

Actually, Anna didn't understand a lot of what other people did or said. Robots were far less complicated. Their actions were functions of a code, not of flawed human logic, or worse, decisions based on emotions.

Yoshi was constantly full of emotions, and no matter how hard he tried to hide them, Anna usually found it easy to figure out what mood he was in just by looking at him. And Anna looked at him a lot. He had nice eyes.

Yoshi turned back to her, catching her mid-stare. Anna quickly glanced away, kicking her foot along the desert floor. It was bone dry, but caked, which suggested water had been here at some point. Now the only river in sight flowed with a thick green liquid that almost seemed to glow. It ran off the hillside and angled leftward, forming a barrier from the rest of the desert. However, a narrow trail ran along the near side of the river. Once the others arrived, that would be their path.

"What now?" Yoshi asked.

"I guess we wait." Anna plunked down on the ground, hoping the sun didn't become any warmer today. There was no shade anywhere in sight.

Yoshi tossed a glance at the sisters, who had settled near some rocks. He grunted something in Japanese that Anna didn't understand, then sat beside her, sending a flutter through her chest.

*Be cool*, she thought, then gave up on that idea. She was a lot of things, but never cool.

"Akiko didn't want to get on the plane," Yoshi said. "She told Kira she had a bad feeling about it, but Kira made her board anyway. And now, for some reason, they're angry at me about it. I didn't even know them until after our plane went down!"

Anna smiled, but said nothing. There probably *was* a reason they were mad at him, but maybe he didn't understand emotions any better than she did.

"I didn't want to get on the flight, either," Yoshi said. He seemed to consider saying more, but he stopped when noises came from up the slope. Footsteps pounded and loose rocks tumbled down the hill. Alarmed voices were calling their names. Kira stood first and spoke to Yoshi, and while they argued in Japanese—again—Anna backed up for a better view above them.

"There you are!" Molly said, scurrying around a ridge of the slope. "Everyone hide!"

"Hide?" Anna asked. "Why?"

"Hide!" Javi said, on Molly's heels with Oliver beside him. "Robots!"

The base of the hill ended with a sheer five-foot jump. Not far away, a flat rock extended from the hillside, creating a small overhang. It would hide them from anything on the slope, although they would be exposed if the robots made it to the desert floor. But it was the best Anna could offer them in the moment.

Molly jumped the last few feet of the slope, followed by Oliver and then Javi. Anna pressed her brows together when she saw Javi. His arms had already been cut by the shredder birds, but something else had gotten to him now.

"Mock-me-birds," Javi said when he caught her looking. "Vicious little beasts. My new archenemies!"

"Molly and I found him half-conscious under a tree," Oliver explained. "He's lucky that he isn't any worse."

"Define worse," Javi said. "I'm in a lot of pain here!"

"And now there are robots?" Anna asked. "Which ones?"

"The same little ones you described to us from the cave." Molly gave one last look up the slope, then joined the rest of her team to crouch beneath the overhang.

The other day, Anna had gone with Yoshi and Kira to explore a cave they'd found in a cliff high above the jungle. Along with the discovery of a holographic map of the rift and a menacing robot with pincers and an apparent instinct to attack humans, they'd stumbled upon an army of brick-sized robots. Those must be the ones Molly was referring to.

"What were the robots doing?" Anna asked.

"Looking for us," Javi said.

They waited, and waited. The tension was thick, like old mechanical oil. Anna didn't understand why Molly and Javi had become so alarmed. From what she had seen, those little robots were harmless, more or less.

Then she saw them. Robots were streaming off the hillside and swarming the desert surface, hundreds of them, all converging at the mouth of the trail she had noticed earlier. Each robot had antennae extended over its square body, carrying rocks that they deposited in a growing pile directly over the trail.

Anna stood taller to get a better look at what they were doing. Was that supposed to be some kind of barricade?

"They were ahead of us on every trail down here," Molly explained. "Each time, they made it impossible to pass."

"We finally had to cut our own trail," Javi said, picking more cactus thorns from his pants.

"This is bad." Yoshi's eyes suggested serious levels of alarm. "I worried those robots would follow us out of the cave. But it's worse than that—they know where we're headed."

"You think they want to stop us from reaching the building?" Molly asked.

"Isn't that obvious?"

It wasn't obvious to Anna. "They're not big enough to stop us," she said. "They're like worker ants—small and single-minded. We could just step on them as we walk by."

Javi's face brightened. "Rob-ants! That's what we'll name them!"

Anna rolled her eyes. "They *work* like ants, but they move more like mites. I'll bet they're great on sand."

"And 'rob-ants' is a terrible name," Yoshi said. "We'll just call them sand mites."

"Yeah, that's way better," Oliver said, and Javi frowned.

"You can name the next thing, Javi," Molly cut in, playing peacemaker.

Anna groaned. Of course there would be a "next thing."

Oliver had been sitting quietly beside Molly, but now he

leaned forward. "It all comes down to whether those robots are good or bad. If they're good, then whatever they're doing might help us reach the building."

Javi turned to Anna, cocking his head sideways. "You're always telling us that you understand robots better than anyone. So what do you think, Anna? Are the mites good or bad?"

Anna swallowed hard. Everyone was looking to her for an answer, but the only thing she was certain of left her stomach in knots: A correct guess might save them all.

But if she was wrong, she could cost the team their lives.

# 5

## Yoshi

**W**hile he waited for Anna's answer, Yoshi turned away from the group long enough to close his eyes and breathe. Anna looked like she was trying to swallow a tire, which told him that any "expert" answer she gave about the robots would only be a wild guess.

The rest of the robotics team was already debating how to interpret the mites' actions.

"What if the building is dangerous?" Molly asked. "Then the mites could be trying to stop us in order to protect us."

"The exact opposite might also be true," Javi said. "If the robots are bad, maybe they don't want us to get to the building because they know we need to be there." He gave Molly's injured shoulder another significant look.

Anna sighed as if she'd been holding her breath too long.

"Robots aren't good or bad! They're only following their program. *That's* our question—who is giving the mites their orders?"

"Maybe we're in some crazy reality show and the robots are being directed by a live voting audience," Oliver said.

"Or we're an experiment," Javi said. "Scientists are testing us to see how we'll react to each new challenge."

"Whoever gave the robots their orders is a monster, nothing less." Yoshi seethed. "If there's a person behind those machines, then he's pure evil, and I've got a torn-up knee and five hundred dead airplane passengers who would agree with me." He noted the shocked reaction from his teammates, but held his ground. "We'd be crazy to trust those things."

Akiko touched Yoshi's arm. "Why are they looking at you like that?" she said in Japanese.

"They want to trust that the robots are helping us," he answered.

"Maybe we should," Kira said. "I think they're keeping the walls of this rift from collapsing. Without them, the arctic ice and water would flood this place."

"You don't know that," Yoshi said.

"We saw them working on the wall, fixing it. There's a reason we named them maintenance robots. Tell the group that!"

"We're calling them sand mites now," Yoshi replied.

"Who cares? Tell them!"

Yoshi sighed, then passed on Kira's message. Anna nodded

in agreement, but then, she was the only other one of the group who had already seen these things in action.

"Kira thinks these robots are keeping us alive?" Oliver asked. "That's a big favor from the same group that probably brought our plane down in the first place."

"They're blocking the trail into the desert," Kira said. "I think they want us to go to the right."

Yoshi looked where she was pointing. It was true. The sand mites seemed to be clearing rocks to form a new path off to the right. If the team went in any other direction, they'd either have to scale the large mound of rocks ahead or cross the green-goo river to the left.

"Where do you think that new trail goes?" Akiko asked.

"Back up the hill," Yoshi said, nodding at the line of robots farther ahead. "They want us to turn around."

His natural defiance rose inside him. If the robots wanted him to go back, then he was determined to go forward. He'd climb a pile of rocks twice as high as what they'd built, or simply use the device to jump over it. He'd do anything but follow the orders of some little brick with mechanical whiskers and legs.

Oliver turned back to the group. "You're right, Yoshi. It's not only the robots we should worry about. I don't trust whoever programmed them."

"Neither do I," Molly said. "We shouldn't trust anything we find in this rift until we have evidence otherwise."

"Then we might be missing out on a lot of help!" Anna said. "We were chosen to survive that crash—all of us felt something save us. Why would they save us and then try to kill us once we landed?"

"I trust them," Akiko said to Yoshi. "If they wanted to harm us, they'd have attacked us already. They must know we're here."

Yoshi nodded, then turned to the group. "Akiko agrees with me. We don't trust them."

Molly glanced doubtfully at Akiko, then looked over at Javi. "What do you think?"

Javi considered his answer a moment, then said, "I like robots. That's not helpful, I know, but I just like them."

Yoshi leaned in. "We're the Killbot team, right? Then I say we go kill us some bots."

Anna shook her head. "That's not the reason for our name."

"Well, it should be! You saw the way that pincer robot went after us in the cave. The only reason we survived was because we turned on the heavy gravity and brought an avalanche down on its head. What will we do if one comes at us across the flat desert floor? No desert I've ever seen is going to spawn an avalanche!"

Anna opened her mouth, but no words came out. Yoshi knew he was right about the avalanche and about the pincer bots. They had bragged plenty about how tough their soccer-playing robot was, but it was nothing compared to the technology she'd seen in that cave. And that said something about whoever had built this whole environment.

*Someone* had designed it. Someone had trapped them here. And they were undoubtedly more advanced than the entire Killbot team put together.

Javi must have been thinking about their soccer-playing robot, too. It had been in a makeshift backpack he had fashioned out of a flannel shirt he'd found among the plane wreckage. Now he withdrew it and set it on the ground. A toaster on wheels—that was how Javi had described it to Yoshi.

"We're programmers," Javi began. "We told this robot to kick a ball and to destroy any other robots who tried to get the ball. We did a good enough job that some international competition wanted to see our work. So why don't we just change this little guy's programming? Tell it to treat those bug robots like a soccer ball."

Anna scoffed. "Well, there is the problem of it being completely broken!"

"For now," Molly said slyly. "It could be fixed, if we had the right parts."

Yoshi smiled. "If we could capture a sand mite, maybe we could salvage it for the right parts."

Anna shook her head. "You got mad when I *kicked* one of them in that cave. Now you want to capture one and rip it apart?"

"I say we do it," Molly said. "We need the parts, and

besides, dismantling one of them might teach us a lot about whoever built them in the first place."

Yoshi stood and rubbed his hands together, then instantly regretted being so eager. Just in the time they had been considering the soccer-playing robot, the number of mites ahead of them had doubled or even tripled in number. He felt like a fly in a den of spiders.

They were doing more than barricading the trail now. They were erasing it, making it seem like the only reasonable path was back up the hill.

Molly stood beside him. "They don't want us crossing that sand. We know that for sure."

Then Anna stood. "And I'm sure that if we try to steal one of them, there's gonna be consequences."

"We'll deal with them. Together." Yoshi spoke with confidence, but he had major doubts. If they were about to start a fight, then he just hoped it was a fight they had any chance of winning.

# 6

## Javi

Javi volunteered to capture the robot.

Why him?

Maybe because he had gone crazy in the jungle, that was why. Maybe because Yoshi had a big sword and a bigger ego, and Javi just wanted to prove that he could do some of the tough-guy stuff, too.

But neither of those was the reason.

It was because Molly had also volunteered, and he didn't want her to go. She pretended that the wound on her shoulder was fine, but it wasn't fine. The last thing she needed was to stir up some robots.

Who was he kidding? That was the last thing any of them needed! Yoshi had a bandage around his knee and walked with a limp, especially when he thought no one was looking. Everyone who'd been in the plane fire had minor burns, and the skin on Javi's arms was a checkerboard of cuts and bites. If he ever came across another mock-me-bird, he'd . . . well, he'd invite it to dinner. As the main course.

"Just grab a bot and go!" Anna called from behind him.

Yes, but which one? Were they all identical, or did they have differences based on their unique duties? Maybe Anna was right and it didn't matter. Nothing was gained by standing out here among them.

The sand mites weren't large. They were significantly smaller than the Killbots' soccer robot. Anna had described the cave mites with eight legs beneath their frames, but these also had roller wheels, far better suited for traveling on sand. They didn't have hands, but each robot had a pair of whiskers that could extend and grab and work like a hand would.

Like a hand . . . or like tanglevine. A disquieting thought.

As numerous as the mites had seemed while he was with his teammates beneath the overhang, that was nothing compared to how it looked now that he was walking among them, tiptoeing with every step to avoid their whiskers. There were more robots here than he could count, and trying to estimate their numbers only made his heart pound worse than it already was.

They continued working as if he weren't there, erasing the trail beneath his feet and replacing it with more rocks, more barriers into the desert. Those that weren't creating an alternate trail up the hillside were widening the green-goo river. Wading through it definitely wasn't an option. When the robot whiskers touched the goo, it ate away at the metal. If the goo dissolved metal, Javi could only imagine what it'd do to human skin.

Each robot continued working without interruption, just like ants, no matter what they had named them.

Javi remembered once hearing that an ant could carry fifty times its weight, the equivalent of him carrying five thousand pounds over his head. He had the sudden image of these robots carrying *him* aloft, back to their evil programmer boss. He *really* didn't want to think about that.

The mites were in constant motion, and though their movements were orderly, Javi couldn't take everything in at a glance. He focused on one robot in particular as it made its way forward with its stone. Once the robot deposited its rock on the growing pile, it turned right, using its whiskers to smooth out the new trail ahead. Orderly. Deliberate. Just like an ant trail.

"Hurry!" Molly hissed from behind him.

Well, that was fine for her. The robots probably didn't even know she was there. They were definitely aware of him, though. They hadn't attacked . . . yet. But he was getting nervous.

"Hey, Javi, let us know when you've got one," Yoshi hissed. "Until then, I'm gonna take a nap."

Javi made a face at him, then turned his attention back to the sand mites. Crouching in position to run, he picked up the one he'd been watching and tucked it under his arm.

It didn't like that. The mite wrapped its whiskers around Javi's arm, squeezing tightly, pinching off the blood flow to his hand.

"Argh!" Javi shouted. He tried to drop the bot, but now it was entangled past his elbow, so he started shaking his arm, dancing around wildly to force it to let go.

It did, but only after he shook it so hard that he ended up falling onto his backside, already sore from the cactus. He yelped in a totally undignified way.

Javi was sure he heard laughter coming from beneath the overhang. He hoped they were enjoying this, because he definitely didn't think this was funny. He was having a bad day.

Or a bad week.

He jumped to his feet and picked up a new bot, this time in both hands with the legs downward and whiskers facing away from him. Its legs wiggled as if it was still walking, then they shuddered and went still.

That was better. Javi turned and took a step toward his friends, but stopped again when a giant thud shook the desert floor.

As a rule, any thud large enough to shake the ground had to be bad. He turned, slowly, dreading to discover what might have been the cause.

Every sand mite that had been carrying a stone piece had dropped it, hundreds of large rocks all landing at the exact same time. The bots had frozen in place, and every metal whisker in the valley was pointed in his direction.

They didn't have eyes, but Javi had the sinking suspicion that they were all looking right at him. A chill ran up his spine.

Slowly, Javi began backing up, the captured robot still in his hands. Then he stopped. The other mites were following, closing in around him on all sides, abandoning their orderly paths as their whiskers extended like long, skinny arms reaching out for him.

Arms that could probably snap him in half.

"Don't just stand there, Javi!" Molly yelled. "Run!"

Yes, obviously he should run, but which way? Back up the steep hill, on the new trail? No, that was what they wanted, and *they* didn't seem very friendly right now.

Should he try scaling the mound of rocks? They'd overtake him in only a few steps. He wasn't about to dive into the green river. He was desperate, but not stupid.

As the sand mites surrounded him, Javi kicked at anything within range, using the one in his hands like a battering ram when necessary. But there were too many, and as soon as one figured out where he was going, they all shifted course to follow him, keeping him surrounded.

Keeping him trapped.

"What should I do?" Javi shouted. "Guys? Hello?"

There was no answer. Javi didn't dare turn around. The mites were closing in so thick, he'd never escape on his own.

Where had his friends gone?

# 7

## Anna

As soon as Javi's robot theft turned sour, Molly had ordered everyone back onto the hillside for their safety.

"Javi needs help!" Anna cried.

Molly was already working on her device, so Anna pulled hers out as well. "Dial it to low tech," Molly said. "Let's turn those things off."

"The last time you experimented with tech, I seem to recall an exploding airplane," Yoshi said.

Molly barely glanced up as she adjusted her disk's settings. "That was the high-tech setting, which raised the plane's capabilities beyond its limits. This is different."

"Maybe tech isn't the right setting to use," Oliver said. "Why don't we just do a low-grav jump over to Javi and pull him out?"

"Because of the wind, obviously." Anna made no effort to hide her annoyance with Oliver and Yoshi for second-guessing the plan. Javi needed help, and this was their best solution.

"Ready?" Molly waited for Anna's nod, then said, "Go."

Simultaneously, the two girls powered on their devices and a massive winding down sound echoed toward them, like the sudden silence in a house when the power goes out.

Javi craned his head around until he found them again and gave a wide smile.

"Told you it'd work," Anna said to Yoshi and Oliver.

Javi started toward them, playfully kicking a sand mite out of his path.

That was a mistake. The instant he kicked it, it exploded, knocking Javi to the ground. Where he landed, other small explosions ignited, leaving enough smoke around Javi that Anna couldn't see him anymore. More explosions rippled from the area in a domino effect.

"They self-destruct in low tech," Molly cried. "Turn it up again, turn them back on!"

Each exploding machine was sending metal debris into the air. If any of that debris hit Javi—

Anna powered up the device and the robots buzzed to life again. Still lost in the smoke, Javi cried, "Make up your minds! Whatever you did nearly blew me up. Now you undid it and they're mad!"

Anna started to point out that robots were not capable of

becoming mad, but she was interrupted by Yoshi, who ran into the fray. "I've had enough of those devices," he said. His sword remained sheathed at his side, but he was clearly eager for a fight. Oliver and the sisters followed, kicking aside robots, or grabbing them and turning them onto their backs, where their wheels spun around uselessly in the air. The randomness of the Killbot attack created confusion among the robots. They seemed unable to determine where to focus their attention.

"I'll get Javi," Molly said to Anna as they loaded the devices back into their backpacks. "We're not taking the mites' trail. Find us the best way into the desert."

But they'd only taken a few steps before Oliver yelled, "Pincer!"

Everyone turned to see a pincer robot making its final descent off the slope. Anna gulped. She had seen one of these things in action.

Pincer robots were much larger than the sand mites, and the pincers that served as their hands were lined with teeth, making it clear what they were designed to do. The machine also had four powerful legs that left deep impressions in the ground, even in this hardened clay, which told Anna how heavy it must be. Like the mites, it had no head, but this one did have a light on the front that seemed to function as an eye. Or, for all she knew, it was a laser, or a camera through which its programmer could watch them. Study them.

That creeped her out, big time.

"We have to cross the river!" Molly yelled. Javi was with her, his face smeared with ash.

The river was too wide to simply step over, and everyone was too spread out to jump with the help of the devices. They'd have to gather near the edge of the river before they could attempt it.

Anna shouted out for everyone to run, and the team followed her, each of them dodging the mites that tried to trip them with every step.

"Get that stupid bot to the other side!" Yoshi yelled at Javi. "If you don't, then all of this stupidity was for nothing!"

Ignoring the fact that Yoshi had just insulted the group's plan—and insulted robots in general—Anna angled toward Javi, to help him if necessary. Yoshi was right. Javi had to get his captive safely across.

Kira was the first to break through the robots, and she held Akiko's hand to pull her along. Molly had been gripped around her ankle by a sand mite, but now it was only bouncing along behind her as she ran.

Anna pushed forward to Javi, shoving him toward the river. He resisted at first, shouting, "Stop! That's acid, Anna!"

"Yes, and I have a device!"

Now he ran with her, though it was easier to dodge the robots than she had expected. Too easy. Despite the fact that Javi was still holding a captured robot, most of them were veering toward Oliver.

Molly must have noticed it, too. She had dived back into

the sea of robots, trying to clear the ones that were gathering around Oliver.

"Kick them!" she shouted. "Like Javi did."

"I can't!" he cried. "There's too many!"

"Do it!" Anna yelled. Maybe Oliver didn't realize how close the pincer robot was to him. Both pincers were extending outward from the robot's frame, and if they clamped down on Oliver, they would do some serious damage.

Molly grabbed a few rocks from the ground and threw them at the pincer robot, but they only bounced off it without even leaving a mark on the metal.

Next she picked up one of the mites and threw that. A pincer intercepted it, snapping it in half with one pinch.

Anna gulped. It had cut through metal like it was a sheet of paper!

At least Molly had slowed the pincer robot, so she picked up other mites and tossed them, too, which finally gave Oliver the opening he needed to run toward her.

As soon as Oliver got close enough, Molly grabbed his arm and pressed the button of her device, then they jumped, the sand mite still dangling from her leg. She finally kicked it off as she tried to steer them toward the river. Hopefully not *into* the river.

By then, Anna had gathered the rest of the team. The pincer robot was advancing on them far too quickly. There was no time to tie everyone together. "Okay, everyone get a hand on the device and jump on three," she said. "One, two, three!"

*"Matte!"* Kira shouted.

Once on the far side of the river, some of the group collapsed to the ground, exhausted but relieved. Anna turned to Javi, who was wrestling with the captured bot, trying to find an off switch. She and Oliver joined in to help him.

Kira and Akiko were chattering in rapid Japanese, their voices in high alarm. Kira finally grabbed Molly's arm and spoke one word: "Yoshi."

Everyone stopped and looked around. He hadn't crossed the river with Molly and Oliver. Panic filled her chest. How had she missed him?

"Where's Yoshi?" Javi asked.

Anna found him first, facing off against the pincer robot near the base of the hill. Taunting it, really, with personal insults such as, "Your mother was a mailbox." It was clever— sort of—but not the kind of strategy a person would use if they understood anything about robot programming. Robots didn't respond to threats or challenges. They responded to their code. Nonetheless, the robot was slowly advancing on him.

"What are you doing?" Molly yelled at him.

"Testing it!" Yoshi replied. "We need to know what this thing can do."

"That *thing* can snap you in half," Anna shouted. What else mattered?

"I'm going to try breaking it," Yoshi said. "We might need to know how to do it in the future."

"No, Yoshi!" Molly shouted. "Get over to this side of the river, now!"

Yoshi only smiled back as he picked up a large rock and hefted it at the robot. It hit the robot directly but bounced off as if Yoshi had thrown a tennis ball. He stepped back from the pincers, keeping just out of their reach.

"I gave you an order," Molly said.

"I don't do orders." Yoshi looked over at her as he spoke, which was a mistake. He tripped over one of the rocks left behind by the mites and fell to his back. A pincer reached for his leg and snapped just as Yoshi pulled it away.

He rolled to his feet and began running for the team. "On second thought," he said, "I deeply respect your leadership, Molly. An order is an order."

"The river is too wide; he won't make it." Anna raised her device, ready to turn on low grav and get Yoshi, but another gust of wind was blowing now. She wouldn't be able to control her jump.

As he ran, Yoshi withdrew his sword, turning it around so that he was holding the blade. "Someone had better catch this and help pull me across," he shouted.

At the edge of the river, he leaped, holding the sword out. Anna was still holding the device. The sisters hadn't understood Yoshi's instructions. Oliver looked frozen, and Javi was moving toward Yoshi, but wouldn't make it in time.

Molly reached out and grabbed the sword's handle as it came toward her, giving a hard enough yank that it pulled

Yoshi across the river. The tip of his shoe dipped into the green goo, and he quickly pulled it out as if stung. The stuff had eaten a hole through his shoe, and continued to eat the leather until he wiped it off on the dirt. Javi was right. The goo was acidic.

"Acid snot!" Javi shouted. "I named it! I get credit for the name!"

"Your mom would be proud," Yoshi said, wiggling his bare toe through the front of the shoe. "Thanks for grabbing me, Molly." Then he looked around and his tone soured. "And thanks, everyone else, for forgetting me."

Anna looked over at Molly, who was bent over with her hands on her knees, catching her breath. That had been close. Too close. And they were only getting started.

# Molly

**M**olly wasn't about to share this with the group, but when she'd pulled Yoshi across the river, she'd felt a surge of strength within her shoulder—and not her healthy, uninjured shoulder. The other one. The infected one.

What was happening to her?

There wasn't time to think about that now.

The pincer robot remained on the opposite side of the—she hated to even think the words, but it was too late—the opposite side of the acid snot, pincers outstretched and snapping. It was impossible for a robot to feel emotions, but this one looked angry.

Team Killbot gathered around the captured sand mite. "I have rope," Anna offered, digging into her backpack. They wound it around the metal whiskers, still waving through the air, trying to attach itself to someone's arm or leg. When the whiskers were secured, the robot was tied onto Anna's backpack.

Meanwhile, Molly scanned the horizon. From what she recalled of the view higher on the hill, they probably had a half mile or more of the hard clay soil before it turned to sand. The sun was already hot and its reflection off this solid ground made the air feel even warmer, and drier. Jumping in low gravity wouldn't be easy, but it'd be far better than walking. She passed out the bungee cords again, asking everyone to hook themselves in.

"What now, Great Leader?" Javi asked. "The sand mites obviously didn't want us to come this way."

Molly stared forward. The building was somewhere far ahead of them—very far, no doubt—but it seemed like their only hope. Neither of the options to her left or right offered anything better. "We have a plan, and we should stick to it."

It wasn't necessarily a great plan, but when you ran out of options, making decisions became easy.

"Let's try to jump together this time," Anna suggested. "We won't all fit on the same tether, but if Oliver and Kira hold hands, we won't get separated again."

Oliver blushed. "Uh, why us?" he aked.

"Because you're on the ends and you're not holding the devices, obviously."

Molly grinned at Anna's logic. "Good plan. Let's jump."

At the highest point in their arc, Molly surveyed the desert again. It was much bigger than she'd expected. It'd be dark soon. They'd have to spend at least one night down below. Just the thought of that sent a shudder through her.

"Can we talk about the attack?" Anna asked, though it wasn't a question, just a statement of what she intended to do. "We learned a lot about the maintenance robots back there."

"Like what?" Yoshi asked.

"Did you see what happened when Javi picked up one of them? They all stopped what they were doing at exactly the same time. And when they moved again, they all did exactly the same thing!"

"So someone *is* directing their actions," Yoshi mused.

"Maybe," Javi said. "But it's more likely the robots are networked—that they have some way of communicating with each other. They don't have eyes or a mouth, so it's something internal."

"Like robot Wi-Fi," Yoshi said. "Silent group texting."

Molly smiled. If that was the way he wanted to think of it, then that was close enough.

"The pincer robot is like their bodyguard," Javi said. "It's protecting the littler ones."

"We don't know that for sure," Anna said. "We know that wherever the mites are, the pincer robot is probably nearby, too. But every time Molly threw a sand mite at it, those pincers clipped it in half. So I don't know if it's protecting them, or following them to get closer to us. That's the dangerous robot. The rest are just annoying."

"Annoying is when the kid sitting behind you in class is smacking his gum," Javi said. "Those things attacked us!"

"After we stole one of them," Anna countered. "We started the fight."

They drifted to the ground, and Molly counted off their next jump. Javi was a little off, but the group pulled him along. This was slower than she'd hoped, and hard on their legs.

She was still fixated on the robot skirmish. There was a final detail they hadn't discussed. Molly didn't even really want to talk about it. But Oliver apparently did.

"Dangerous or not, they're creepy," Oliver said. "Even without eyes, it's pretty obvious when they're looking at you . . . looking at *me*. Did you notice? It was like they were after me in particular."

Molly hated it, but Oliver was right. They had definitely locked on to him. Even with Javi carrying a captured bot in his arms, it had been more important to them to surround Oliver.

"Why you?" Anna asked. "No offense, but there are better engineers on the team, and you're the youngest."

"Which means what, exactly?" Molly intended to take offense at that, even if Oliver wouldn't. "He earned his way onto our team, just like everyone else, and whatever chose us to survive the crash, it chose Oliver, too. If the robots noticed him, then there's a reason for it!"

Silence followed, until Yoshi muttered, "Congratulations, kid." It was a stark reminder that being singled out here wasn't exactly a badge of honor.

Molly didn't say it, but she worried that it was *because* Oliver was the youngest that he had been targeted. Had the robots identified him as a weak link—as prey? It was her fault he was here in the first place. She'd convinced his parents he was integral to the team. And she's promided to keep him safe.

They continued flying, or high-bouncing, until the first of the moons rose against the white sky. It was a red moon, eerie but beautiful.

"I've got a theory," she told them. "About the colors in this place."

Javi gave her a funny look. "The colors?"

"Have you noticed? Everything that's attacked us so far—everything natural, I mean—has been green."

"I'm not sure anything here is natural, exactly," Javi countered.

"You know what I mean. Robots aside, what have we been up against? The shredders are green. So was the tanglevine. The duck."

Oliver looked over at Anna. "What do you think?"

Anna thought for a moment. "It's not impossible. Color can be very meaningful in nature. Yellows or reds can signal danger."

Yoshi seemed intrigued. He fired off a translation for the sisters.

"So it's mixed up here?" Javi asked. "At home, green means go, red means stop."

"Think of it this way," Molly said. "Here in the rift, green means 'go ahead and die if you're near it.'"

"Green," Akiko said. "*Midori.*"

"*Midori,*" Molly repeated. "*Midori* is bad."

"Bad . . . *midori,*" Akiko said. "Red. *Aka.*"

"*Aka* is good," Molly said. "Red means, 'stop fighting me and just relax already!'"

Javi chuckled. "What about blue?"

Molly hadn't quite figured out blue yet. Everyone else seemed to have liked the blue berries from the jungle, but she didn't. To her, they just tasted wrong.

"Blue," Kira said. "*Ao.*"

The group repeated the word. Kira and Akiko smiled at each other, then at everyone around them. It wasn't much, but it was three more words they could share.

"Anyway, it's just a theory," Molly said. "We can see if it pans out."

This was basic scientific method. Develop a theory and then experiment to test that theory. However, while that worked fine in a robotics lab, this was real life. It bothered her to realize how much could be riding on this hunch of hers being correct.

Oliver let out a whoop. "We need to go down!" he shouted. "Everyone, look ahead!"

*Not more robots*, Molly thought with a groan, but that wasn't it. A handful of boxes were scattered across the ground. Was that luggage?

When their plane had been torn apart, objects from the plane would naturally have flown out, but Molly never expected to find anything so far from the crash site. Then again, the crash hadn't exactly followed the laws of physics. There weren't many suitcases, only five or six, but each one potentially held a survivor's treasure. They had to know what was inside!

When they touched down, Anna and Javi each rotated the devices to turn on the gravity again. Although Molly didn't usually like the additional weight that came with the end of a flight, she was far too eager to check out those bags to care about the sudden pit in her gut.

They disconnected from the bungee cords, and everyone grabbed a bag for investigation. Javi took the largest one, stuffed so full it had needed a rope around the outside to keep it together. Molly grabbed one slightly smaller with hard sides that had taken a considerable beating. Yoshi was walking away from the rest of the group to open the one he'd chosen, plain black with only a line of red duct tape marking the top. He was clearly in a mood, perhaps dwelling on the people who'd packed these bags and were now gone. She'd give him space, so long as he didn't stray too far.

"Pure gold!" Javi said, bringing her attention back to the others. He was raising up a bulk-size bag of candy. "Who feels like a snack?"

# 9

# Yoshi

Yoshi heard the others celebrate the large bag of candy and then heard Molly say everyone could take only three, because she was confiscating the rest for rationing. Based on their response, it wasn't a popular decision, but that's what made Molly a good leader. She didn't make her decisions for popularity. She was doing what she thought was right for the team. He respected that.

He wished he were more like that, too. Stealing his father's sword to take it to America was hardly an act of honor. It was flat-out rebellion. And as it turned out, because the sword was a historic national treasure, his first major act of rebellion also happened to risk an international incident. That figured.

If he did get out of this rift alive, would his crime be forgiven? Maybe Japan would say, "Hey, you were in a plane crash, survived that bizarre wilderness with its seriously nasty predators, and used a stolen sword to save a lot of lives. You've already been punished enough."

Yeah, maybe that would work for Japan, and it might be his American mother's way to forgive and forget, but his father would be different. Yoshi could apologize a hundred times for taking the sword, and it wouldn't matter. Which was why he didn't intend to apologize even once.

The group must have found something else of value back there. He wasn't sure what it was, but following a brief cheer, Molly confiscated that, too.

Now Yoshi turned to the bag he had grabbed. There was a reason he had chosen this one. It was his.

His name was on the luggage tag. When he'd written it down at the airport, though, he hadn't known which address to put. Should he have used the address where he wanted to be, the place he considered home? Or where he was going? In the end, he had skipped the address. He hadn't really cared if the airline lost his luggage. He hadn't expected the airline to lose him.

"This bag has a lot of papers at the bottom," Molly was saying. "Looks like a lawyer's suitcase. The paper will be great for fire starters. And look! A cell phone."

"I think we're out of texting range," Anna said wryly.

"Sure, but it could still be useful. I'll turn it off, preserve the battery."

"Mine has a cool knife," Javi said. "I'm keeping this. The

rest of the stuff in here is clothes. It'd take four of me to wear any of these shirts."

"Javi, shirt," Akiko said in English.

"*Shatsu,*" Yoshi mumbled under his breath. Not that anyone would hear.

"I'm not wearing that!" Javi shouted. "No way! If there is even a .0001 percent chance that we get rescued, I am not having my picture splashed all over the world in that shirt!"

Yoshi turned around, and even in his grim mood, he found himself smiling. Akiko had found a shirt that looked exactly Javi's size. It was light green and decorated in pink ponies.

"The shirt you've been wearing is being held together by threads," Molly said. "You can't keep wearing it."

"Besides, it smells," Anna said.

"We all smell," Javi said. "I'm not wearing the pink ponies shirt."

Kira began rattling off some excited Japanese. Yoshi understood. She'd found food—roasted seaweed with a soy-sauce spice. He liked it, and he was sure both sisters would, but he wondered how hungry the rest of the team would have to get before they decided to try the green crisps.

Molly, he noticed, didn't attempt to confiscate it. She might not yet even be sure what it was.

Yoshi unzipped his bag. He saw T-shirts, a pair of dress shoes, and some self-help book his mother thought he might want to read on the way over—which he hadn't. It was all familiar to him, of course, and yet his things felt utterly foreign in this place. What good were dress shoes to him now?

His eyes drifted to a white envelope sticking out of the book. It was a sealed letter from his mother to his father, which she had made him promise to deliver unopened.

Yoshi had intended to keep that promise, but what did it matter now? Their chances of getting out of this place weren't good, no matter how optimistic Molly pretended to be. He would never have the chance to deliver that letter.

Yoshi ripped open the envelope, but held the letter closed between his fingers. Did his promise to his mother still matter? He had his flaws, but breaking promises wasn't one of them. On the other hand, Team Killbot was rummaging through those other passengers' things without a thought for who those people had been, for what secrets their baggage had held. If Yoshi hadn't survived, they'd be going through his bag now, too, just the same way. They'd have already opened this letter and read it.

"This box is pretty valuable," Oliver was saying. "I think it's an emergency survival kit for the pilot. There's a couple of days' worth of food, two emergency blankets, a few more flares, some duct tape, rope, three water bottles, a fishing kit . . ."

"We won't get much fishing done in the desert," Anna said.

"But maybe it'll be useful ahead," Molly said. "Good job, everyone. Let's pack everything we can carry. We'll have to leave the rest behind." Then she called over to Yoshi. "Find anything useful?"

He ignored her and unfolded the letter. It was signed by his mother and addressed to his father. This alone was significant. His parents' divorce had been anything but friendly, with his father accusing his mother of only wanting Yoshi because it would entitle her to more money, and she accusing him of making Yoshi a pawn in their negotiations. The court had ordered his parents to send all further communications through their lawyers.

So if she was writing his father directly, that was big.

*Our son is often in trouble here*, his mother had written. *He says he's too Japanese to fit in with Americans, and too American to return to Japan.*

There was truth to that, though his father would only tell him to grow up and stop complaining about his heritage. That would be followed by an endless lecture about noble bloodlines and honor and his responsibility to his family, and whatever else his father would say once Yoshi had tuned out entirely.

*Yoshi needs to find himself,* his mother continued. *He needs to figure out who he really is. I think he needs a new adventure.*

Like surviving a plane crash and carnivorous plant life? Was that enough of an adventure for her?

Then in the final paragraph, she wrote, *I cannot control Yoshi anymore. I'm asking you to keep him in Japan, permanently.*

*Permanently.*

The word rang out like a hammer in Yoshi's head. She wasn't sending him back to Japan to resolve the incident with the sword, or because it was his father's turn for custody. She was sending him there because she wanted to get rid of him. Permanently.

"Are you all right?" Kira called to him. "You're really quiet."

Yoshi didn't respond, because responding would have required him to speak Japanese, and he wasn't in the mood for that. He crumpled up the letter and stuffed it into his pocket. If Molly wanted paper for a fire starter, he would gladly provide it.

So he could not be controlled? If his mother thought that was true before, then she should see him in the rift. Because he had no intention of letting anyone control him here. Not the robots, or their programmer, or even Molly with all her positive-attitude leadership. No one told him what to do.

Yoshi stuffed some clothes and his toothbrush into his backpack, and returned to the group. He didn't care about anything else he was leaving behind. As far as he was concerned, none of it mattered anymore.

Javi looked beyond ridiculous in his pink ponies shirt. "Look what they made me wear!" he said when he saw Yoshi. "Did you find anything better in the bag you were looking in?"

"No." Yoshi looked at Molly. "If you're all finished scavenging from the dead, then let's go. It'll be dark soon, and I'm in the mood to go hunting."

# 10

## Anna

Anna knew Yoshi was upset—all the Killbots knew it, but nobody understood why, and he certainly wasn't talking.

Kira kept asking him questions in Japanese and he ignored almost all of them. If only Anna could speak Japanese. Even knowing Kira's questions might help her understand what was bothering Yoshi so much.

When a computer program didn't work, you had to go through the code and find the error. It didn't have to be big. One little typo could shut the whole system down.

People had to be the same way. They follow whatever system has been coded into them, based on their history and training, and the experiences they've gone through. If they shut down, it could be due to the tiniest glitch, something that would seem insignificant to everyone else.

All Anna had to do was find the error in Yoshi's coding.

Molly and most of the other Killbots had stayed back to get an overnight shelter set up, to try to build a fire, and if there was time, to scavenge their captured maintenance robot for parts. When Yoshi and Kira had left camp to look for food, Anna came along to find water. But Yoshi wasn't making it easy. He kept moving toward higher ground.

"We need to go downhill," Anna said. "You know, the direction water runs?"

"Then go downhill." Yoshi scowled. "Kira and I need to get to the top of this hill to look for anything worth eating."

Actually, if they found water, like Anna wanted, they would probably also find some sort of animal in the area. But she didn't feel like arguing with Yoshi. He was in the kind of mood where she knew he'd win the argument, even if he was wrong.

The hill they climbed wasn't large. The mesas in the distance were taller and the walls of the rift had been even taller still. But it did give them a nice view of their route for the next day.

*Nice* might be the wrong word. Nothing ahead looked *nice*.

The same bloodred sand that had been only a small outcrop when they first entered the desert now stretched out as far as she could see. They'd have no choice but to cross it.

Kira said something to Yoshi. When Anna looked at him for a translation, he sighed and said, "She thinks it looks like a red ocean. If you look carefully, you can see places where the sand moves, like waves."

Moving sand? That couldn't be good.

"Maybe it's just the light." Anna glanced up at the red moon, which was climbing higher into the sky. Before long, it'd be dark out.

Yoshi looked up at the moon, too. "That might affect the color of the sand, but not whether it moves. Don't fool yourself—something is not right out there."

"Blood sand," Anna said. "That'll be its name."

Yoshi nodded solemnly.

"Shh." Kira held up her hand.

They went silent. Somewhere nearby was a clicking sound, like insect wings clapping together, or the touch of a talon on rock. Something close to them was alive, and moving.

Anna shivered. Her family had once taken her on a vacation to Florida. The insects there were different from those in New York—larger, and some of them very aggressive. But as a biology geek, she'd found them fascinating. Something told her that whatever was causing the sound now would also be fascinating, but also a lot more threatening. And the sounds were growing more numerous. Louder.

Yoshi flinched. It took Anna a moment to realize it wasn't in response to the noises. She looked down and saw that she had grabbed his hand. She immediately released it and felt her face turn colors that would rival the blood sand.

She couldn't explain why she had done that, not even to herself. Better to say nothing and hope Yoshi forgot it had ever happened.

Luckily, Kira called over to Yoshi, and even if Anna couldn't understand the words, she knew Kira's meaning. She had found a trail. The tracks on it were large. Four paws with a tail that dragged in the dirt behind it.

Kira and Yoshi looked at her as if she was supposed to know what creature had created this. Anna only shrugged, then said, "All I can say is an animal this size probably needs water to survive. If we follow its trail, we'll find some."

And probably find the animal. Anna did not say that. She didn't need to.

Yoshi put a finger to his lips, then withdrew his sword and took the lead along the trail. Kira followed close behind him. At the rear of the group, Anna looked up and saw the green moon beginning its rise, almost as if it wanted to chase the red moon away.

Anna wished Yoshi were next to her now. She would've taken his hand without apologizing. She didn't like being at the end of their line.

The trail meandered downhill, all the while bearing the same paw prints as before.

"This might not lead to water," Anna muttered. "It might take us to this animal's den. Or if it's an intelligent creature, this might be a trap."

"Kira's lucky she can't understand you," Yoshi said. "I wish I couldn't, either."

"I'm just warning you to keep your sword ready," Anna said. Yoshi took about ten more steps around a bend, then said, "Well, look at this. I guess we found water. If you can call it that."

Anna pushed forward to see it, too. It wasn't what she had hoped for, but about what she had expected. Something had stamped a hole deep into the ground, about as round as a pancake. Water had collected within it, where, in the shade of the hillside, it probably didn't evaporate as quickly as it otherwise would. The water was brown, though, covered with a sheen of dust, and almost certainly contained weird bacteria that would make them grow horns or something. That'd be some crazy scientific experiment.

"We'll have to boil it," she told Yoshi. "I hope the others got a fire started."

Kira and Anna began collecting water with the empty bottles they had brought. There would only be enough to fill a couple of bottles, but if none of them died from drinking the dirty water tonight, Anna figured they could come back in the morning and the hole should have refilled.

While they worked, Yoshi pushed his sword through the thin grasses around them. That clicking sound was even louder down here.

"Keep your eyes open for trouble," he said. "No sudden movements."

Kira looked up at him with wide eyes. Anna nudged her to return to filling the bottles. Once the water in the hole was gone, they could screw on the lids and get out of here. The darker it became, the creepier this little watering hole got.

Suddenly, something hissed from the grasses.

"Get down!" Yoshi cried.

Anna and Kira lowered their heads, covering them with their arms. Anna peeked sideways to see Yoshi leap into the air and spin, wielding the sword like she'd only ever seen done in the movies. In that single spin, at least three . . . things . . . fell to the ground. Two more flew at him, which he killed by striking the blade forward for the first, and backward for the second.

Then it was silent.

"I'd say that counts as a sudden movement," Anna said. "But in a good way."

Yoshi smiled, looking genuinely proud of himself, and maybe a little embarrassed. "Thanks."

Anna finished screwing on the lid of her water bottle and then crouched beside Yoshi to stare at the creatures.

Each one was about as large as her fist, but long and narrow with a shell over its body. It had eight legs, two front pincers, and a curling tail with a stinger on the end.

"Scorpions," Yoshi said.

"But look!" Anna pointed to the scorpion's legs. The hindmost legs were larger and longer than those in the front. "These are built like a grasshopper's legs, for jumping, not walking."

"Flying scorpions?" Yoshi shook his head. "Not cool, rift. Not cool at all."

"Let's take these back with us," Anna said. "I'd like to study them. And . . . well, they might be edible."

A fire was burning by the time they returned. It wasn't much, but Anna was hungry enough that even launch scorpions, as she'd decided to call them, sounded delicious.

They poured the water into Yoshi's metal canteen to boil, and then Anna explained what they had seen of the blood sand and launch scorpions while Yoshi and Javi dissected the scorpions for their meat.

"Blood sand?" Oliver asked. "Who named it blood sand?"

"I did," Anna said.

"It couldn't have been cherry lollipop sand, or red roses sand? It had to be—"

"Blood sand," Yoshi said. "Nobody's going to respect cherry lollipop sand, and trust me, this sand will demand that you give it respect."

While the scorpion meat cooked, Anna inspected the stinger on one's tail. "What do you suppose happens to someone who gets stung?" she asked.

Javi shrugged. "My uncle was stung by a scorpion once. It hurt a lot, but he didn't die. Some scorpions have enough toxin to kill a person, though."

"We probably need to find out what these do," Anna said. "We had a volunteer test the pukeberries. The easy way of finding out what happens is to have a volunteer—"

"No!" everyone shouted.

Anna only sighed. If they didn't want to test the scorpions the easy way, then she had a feeling the Killbots would get their answer the hard way. And that could be much worse.

# 11

# Javi

When Yoshi, Anna, and Kira had left camp to go hunting for food and water, Javi's attention had immediately turned to their soccer robot. Molly and Oliver eagerly joined him. They gestured to Akiko that she should help them, too, but she only smiled and reached for her flute.

"It's more damaged than I thought," Molly said once their robot was opened up. "I hope the bot we captured today has parts we can use."

"Maybe we shouldn't dissect it," Oliver said. "Think of how far we could advance robotics if we brought this back in one piece."

"Think of how far *we* could advance if *we* got back in one piece!" Javi countered. That ended their discussion. They were dissecting the robot.

The technology inside the maintenance robot was completely foreign to Javi. Even Molly, who knew more about robots than almost anyone, couldn't explain a lot of what they were seeing.

"But good science is universal," Javi insisted. "If it works for them, it should work for us." He didn't know if that was true, but it sounded good and was enough justification to start digging for parts.

They replaced the soccer robot's missing wheel with one of the mite's rollers, fixed the wiring, and pounded holes into the frame to insert the metal whiskers, though they didn't move around like they had on the maintenance robot. The whiskers only occasionally gave a halfhearted brush at the air, then flopped back onto the ground.

"Epic fail," Oliver whispered.

Javi pretended not to hear that. "We should swap batteries. I bet the right power source will make the whiskers work."

"Too risky," Oliver said. "The mites are connected to each other somehow. Maybe the battery has something to do with that. We don't want our robot to be taken over by them and turned against us."

"Besides," Molly added, "it's bound to get cold tonight. With our little stack of wood, a fire won't last for long. We can use the battery for heat."

Javi couldn't argue with that. Since the green moon had risen, the air had already cooled off considerably.

He was screwing the back of the frame into place when the rest of their team returned to camp.

"What do you think of Hercules?" he asked them.

"Hercules?" Anna chuckled as she looked over his redesigned kicking toaster. "The Greek demigod known for his strength?"

"Technically, Hercules was his Roman name," Javi corrected. "The Greeks called him Heracles."

"Well, *technically*, don't you think either name overstates what our little robot can do?"

Javi covered the sides of the robot's frame with his hands, where its ears would be if it had any. "You'll hurt its feelings." He knew a statement like that would irritate Anna.

Sure enough, she exclaimed, "Robots don't have feelings!"

"But if they do, your robot looks depressed," Yoshi said, pointing out the limp whiskers. "Maybe you should name it Droopy."

"If I name it Hercules, it'll want to do great things to live up to its name," Javi insisted.

"It can't *want* anything!" Anna was truly frustrated now. "You know all this, Javi!"

"I like the name," Molly said.

That was good enough for Javi. Hercules was its name.

With that settled, the group's attention turned to the results of Yoshi's hunt, such as it was.

"You should've seen the way Yoshi got them!" Anna said proudly. "We call them launch scorpions."

Javi had to admit, that was a cool name. But once they got Hercules onto the blood sand tomorrow and everyone saw the way it protected their group, that'd get his name *and* his robot the respect they deserved.

And although the launch scorpions had a great name, their taste was . . . not great. Javi didn't consider himself picky about food. As far as he was concerned, he'd give anything a chance, as long as it was edible.

But the launch scorpions were only edible in the sense that a person might survive eating them. The meat was like eating chewy cardboard with a sprinkle of manure for seasoning. The taste didn't improve much when Molly supplemented their meal with the Japanese seaweed crackers they'd found in the luggage. Javi figured at least they were better than the scorpions, but Molly and Oliver volunteered their rations, still untouched, to the sisters, who happily ate them up.

Yoshi ate alone, even after Molly invited him to join the group. Javi had tried to buddy up to the guy—really, he had. But Yoshi didn't seem to want friends. Either that, or he wasn't entirely sure how to make them. Javi smiled and picked up Hercules, then walked it over to Yoshi. Plunking down beside his future friend, Javi said, "Want to see how we melded human and rift technology?"

"No."

Something was definitely wrong with Yoshi, then, because as far as Javi was concerned, he could be feeling low enough to crawl under a termite's belly, and if someone offered to show him futuristic technology, that'd totally cheer him up. Yoshi's mind was further away than any excitement this desert could offer.

Javi sighed. "We'll get back home. I'm sure of that."

"Maybe I don't want to get back home," Yoshi muttered.

Javi hesitated only for a second, then said, "Okay, how about this plan? After we're rescued, I promise not to tell anyone you survived. I'll sneak you back to live with my family. My mom won't mind your being there, though you are going to have to forget your love of launch scorpion meat to enjoy her food."

Yoshi smiled, despite clearly trying not to enjoy the joke. It was only half a joke anyway. Javi's mom was an artist in the kitchen.

Javi stood again and clapped Yoshi on the back. "We're getting home, dude, and when we do, you're eating dinner at my house—everyone's invited!"

All of Team Killbot cheered at that, even Kira and Akiko. It made Javi wonder what they thought they were cheering for.

"We should get some sleep," Molly said as the last of their fire finally burned out, sooner than Javi would wish. "We've got maybe seven hours until sunlight. Everyone gets a one-hour watch. Who wants to start?"

Yoshi translated for the sisters, and Kira quickly raised her hand. Javi should've volunteered faster, but the first time he'd volunteered for something, he ended up doing the hokey-croaky with those pukeberries. And the second nearly got him blown up by kamikaze mite bots. Those kind of experiences made him shy about volunteering a third time.

"Okay, Kira needs to watch out for anything dangerous," Molly said. "Yoshi, will you translate that for her?"

"I think she's got the general idea of what a lookout does," Yoshi said.

Molly smiled, looking a little embarrassed. "I guess you're right. We have two batteries for warmth. That's three people per battery, with one person on watch. Everyone huddle in close—sharing body heat is a good thing."

Was it? Javi looked around the group and suddenly felt unsure about who he was supposed to huddle in close with. Akiko came over to Yoshi, and so did Anna. That left Molly, Oliver, and him on the second battery. A small gust of night wind—what did the sisters call it, *yokaze*?—blew through camp, and he shivered. That was enough to make Javi stop caring about huddling in close. He'd be an ice cube by morning if he didn't share some battery heat with his teammates.

He, Molly, and Oliver set their battery in the center of their group, then each pressed in tightly around it, face-first and feet out. The battery didn't put out nearly as much heat as a fire, but it would get them through the night.

Snores immediately came from the other half of their team. Oliver wasn't far behind them in falling asleep. Kira was walking in a steady circle around the perimeter of their camp. Even with his eyes closed, Javi could tell where she was by the crunch of dry dirt beneath her feet.

"Javi, you awake?" Molly whispered.

With his eyes still closed, Javi murmured, "Yes. Why?"

"The blood sand tomorrow. It's making me nervous."

"Anna gave it a scary name. But maybe blood sand is just . . . sand."

"Maybe."

But by the sound of her voice, Javi could tell she didn't believe it. For that matter, neither did he.

Javi whispered, "How's your shoulder?"

In the darkness, he could almost hear her smile. "I feel good; better than I should. And it's strange, because I know it looks infected, but it doesn't hurt at all."

"So you're okay?"

"I'm better than that. I can tell that it's cold out here, but it's not bothering me. And I wasn't all that hungry when we ate, even though I should be starving."

Javi was plenty hungry, even after they'd eaten. It was a good thing Molly was in charge of rationing out the food, because if it was up to him, they'd have devoured everything already. Also, he'd have burned this stupid shirt in the fire, no matter how bad his last shirt had been torn up.

With that, Javi pressed his body even closer to the battery, and fell into a deep sleep.

So deep that when he heard Molly's cry sometime later, he awoke ready to fight. Oliver was on watch now and had looked over at them, but he didn't seem alarmed.

"Molly?" Javi asked.

She was still trying to catch her breath and sweat ran in a bead down the side of her face, which was especially unusual on a cold night like this one.

"It was only a dream," she said. "Nothing to worry about."

"You look worried." Truth was, she looked worse than worried. She looked like she'd just walked through one of those late-night horror movies. It took a lot to rattle Molly's nerves.

"I've got enough real-world problems," Molly said, slicking back her hair to get it out of her face. "I'm not going to stress about some stupid dream."

She could say practical things all night if she wanted, but Javi knew her better than that. Something in the dream was bothering her. And even as she laid down again, he was sure she wouldn't be able to go back to sleep. Of course, neither would he. Not now.

"It's probably time to switch out to a new watch," he told Oliver. "My turn."

Oliver yawned. "That's great, Javi. Thanks for volunteering!"

*Volunteering*, Javi thought. Why did that have to be the last word he heard before starting his hour of being alone in an unfamiliar darkness, now with only a green moon for light?

# 12

## Molly

Morning came sooner than anyone wanted, except for Molly, who had laid awake on the ground without closing her eyes again.

It had only been a dream, so it was ridiculous to let it bother her this much. Especially considering she couldn't remember the details. Those had trickled away from her like water cupped in her hands. Now the dream was gone entirely. And somehow that made it worse. Because the feeling of weight in her chest still remained, a sense of dread about going forward.

She had taken last watch, and as soon as the sun began to warm the ground, she hollered for everyone to wake up. Her teammates could groan all they wanted, but it would only get hotter. They had to start moving.

The water that Anna had located and boiled had cooled

down overnight. Now they distributed it evenly into everyone's water bottles. It came out with a lot of sand—

"Maybe there's good vitamins in there," Molly offered.

—and had a sort of reddish earth tint to it.

"We can pretend it's a cherry drink," she suggested.

"Made with rotten cherries," Oliver said, after taking a sip of his. "Yuck!"

"Get used to it until we find more," Anna said. "And don't waste any because who knows *when* we'll find more."

Molly still had some sealed water containers in her backpack, but she didn't want to use those yet. They had to save them in case they needed clean water, maybe to wash out a wound. She wished she didn't have to think like that.

"Day two of the desert," Javi said optimistically. "The day of the blood sand! How could that not be fun?"

Team Killbot growled back at him, and Yoshi even tossed his socks at Javi before demanding them back so he could put them on.

"I'd say no," Javi laughed, "but, dude, something is seriously wrong with your foot odor!"

"Foot odor," Akiko repeated. "Yoshi."

Molly waited to see what Yoshi would do, but he only sniffed his socks and, with a smile, said, "At least I'm not wearing a shirt with pink ponies on it."

Javi tossed a bungee cord at Yoshi, but it was all in good fun, and Molly decided they needed a little more of that. Wasn't that part of being a good leader—keeping everyone's spirits up?

After they broke camp, Yoshi led the way around the hill that he and Anna and Kira had climbed last night. By the time they got in position to see the valley they were about to enter, the sun was already turning the place into an oven. The blood sand would likely be worse. It stretched out before them now, like a vast red sea.

Red was supposed to be good inside the rift. But Molly knew this wasn't.

Luckily, they had the devices and everyone was already attaching themselves to the bungee cords. It might take them all day and half the night to cross this sand, but she didn't care. They weren't coming down until they were all the way across.

"Devices on," Molly ordered.

She and Anna powered on their devices, and Molly felt the now-familiar hum inside her gut.

"Guys . . ." Javi said.

"Everyone have all their stuff?" Molly asked, digging through her own backpack. "Double-check before we jump."

*"Tatsumaki!"* Kira cried, tugging on Yoshi's arm.

He groaned, then turned sharply toward Molly. "Hey, you ever jumped through a tornado?"

Molly rolled her eyes as she turned to look at what the rest of her team was already staring at. Then her breath caught in her throat.

Massive columns of sand were rising from the desert floor,

swirling in rising circles that pushed the columns higher and higher.

"Are we causing that?" Anna asked. "The low gravity?"

Nobody answered her, including Molly, who couldn't stop staring ahead. The nearest column was only fifty feet away, alarmingly close. It was at least ten feet wide and by now had extended over four stories high. These weren't true tornados, though. They originated from the ground, not the sky, and were wider near their base. The more the sand swirled, the higher it stretched.

"Everyone move back," Molly said, and even Yoshi obeyed this order instantly. With the low gravity, they had an extra bounce in their steps.

"Eighteen, nineteen," Oliver said. "I think I count nineteen columns. Wait! Another one just started."

"I told you those disks are dangerous," Yoshi said. "Turn them off or you'll produce some massive super tornado."

"Agreed," said Molly. "Anna?"

They turned their devices off and saw the columns slow in their rotations. Then Anna said, "Uh-oh."

"Uh-oh?" Yoshi asked. "What do you mean, uh-oh?"

Molly saw the problem. With both devices off, the sand fell back to the earth like it had been poured from the skies. There was so much, and it had been moving so rapidly, the collapse created tidal waves of sand that rushed at them.

"Run!" Javi shouted.

Still attached by the bungee cords, Molly was reminded of the three-legged races she used to play as a child. Oliver was the slowest runner on her cord, but they still outpaced the worst of the sand.

By the time they stopped, they were almost back as far as last night's camp. The hill Yoshi had taken them around looked only half the size it had been before.

Anna sighed. "There goes our water source."

"And we can't use the low gravity," Yoshi said.

No, they couldn't. If their jumps weren't perfectly precise—and they never were—they could too easily get caught up in one of those swirling columns of sand.

While Yoshi translated for Kira and Akiko, Oliver said, "So, we're walking?" He sighed. "By the time we reach the end, I'll be a walking corpse."

"Maybe it's like a mirage," Molly offered. "Where the desert looks bigger than it really is."

"That's not how mirages work," Anna said.

Molly knew that. She was just hoping Oliver didn't.

Oliver squinted ahead. "How do we know the sand is safe to walk on? I mean, after what we just saw?"

"I have an idea!" Javi knelt on the ground and powered Hercules on. He had a remote device to control it, as long as it stayed within range.

"So it'll be our advance team?" Yoshi asked. "Our scout?"

"I don't want our bot to get wrecked," Javi said. "But if

anything dangerous happens out there, it'll happen to Hercules first. Hopefully that'll give us time to get away."

"It's going to trip over its own whiskers," Yoshi said.

"That's my next planned upgrade," Javi said. "It won't trip."

Privately, Molly thought there was a chance Yoshi could be right—it might trip. But Javi had worked hard to get the machine moving. She wouldn't discourage him now.

He crouched to the ground and gave Hercules a dog pat on the top of its frame. "You were meant to get us a trophy," he mumbled. "Now I hope you'll get us home. See you soon, my friend."

"If you want to kiss it good-bye, better hurry," Yoshi said.

Javi only smiled. "I would, but Hercules isn't really my type."

He rechecked Hercules's battery, then set it moving out across the blood sand. Molly held her breath.

"Twenty feet in and all is well, that's good enough for me," Javi said after a minute, stretching out a foot.

Anna grabbed him, yanking him back toward her. "Twenty feet is nothing! Did you know a shark can detect a single drop of blood from three miles away? Just one drop!"

"Uh-huh. So you figure there's a big problem here with desert sharks?" Yoshi asked her. "Spotted any dorsal fins in the sand yet?"

"My point is, we need to give Hercules a little more time, that's all."

At forty feet, Yoshi lost patience. He took two steps in,

paused, and then turned around and smiled. "It's fine. We're wasting time."

The sisters followed him, then Anna, Javi, and Oliver, and Molly went last of all. As soon as her feet touched down on the familiar-feeling sand, she felt foolish. It was like the dream last night—they had enough real problems without her imagination inventing nonexistent threats. *They* had named the sand, so the fact that it sounded so scary was their own fault. Oliver was right. They should have named it cherry lollipop sand.

With Hercules leading them on a straight course forward, Team Killbot began making good progress. It wasn't as fast as flying, but it was better than being sucked into a twister. And nothing could sneak up on them. There was nowhere for anything to hide out here, though that also meant there was nowhere for *them* to hide, either. The only feature to the landscape was an occasional rock, which she supposed could obscure launch scorpions, so she warned the team to stay clear, just in case. But they could do this. No problem.

If only it weren't so hot. The sand soaked up the sun like a hot plate, and within a couple more hours, they would start to fry. Molly reached for her water bottle, tempted to take a drink, but then put it back. She was warm, but not sweating yet. She'd replenish her water after she started to sweat.

Just ahead of her, Anna did reach for her bottle and took a long drink. However, she immediately spat it out. "Blech, too much sand!"

Right beneath her, the sand softened, swallowing her left leg up to the knee.

"What the—?" Anna scowled. "Is this quicksand?"

"Can you get out?" Oliver asked.

Anna put her weight on her right leg and tried to stand up with it. "It's completely solid now. I'm stuck. I need someone to pull me out."

"Did the sand look any different where you stepped?" Molly asked, still keeping her distance. "Are there any other soft patches around you?"

Anna punched on the ground around her, but the sand only reacted as sand should, leaving a little bowl where her fist went down, with individual grains sliding into the center.

"It's safe," Javi said, starting forward.

Anna's eyes widened. "Guys, something just brushed against my leg!"

Javi froze. "What?"

"There's something down there. Something under the sand!"

# 13

## Anna

In tough situations, Anna wasn't the type of person to panic. She was the one who reasoned through the problem, who calculated the odds of success. She was practical and sensible.

And at the moment, she was scared out of her wits. Her heart was pounding as if she'd just run a marathon and her mouth had turned to paste.

"Don't move!" Molly cried.

Anna rolled her eyes. In the first place, her leg was *stuck*! Not being able to move was the problem, not the solution. And in the second place, if Molly had felt the length of the *thing* that brushed against her, the last advice she'd have given was to stay where she was.

"Get me out!" Anna shouted.

"Shh," Yoshi said. "Maybe it can hear you!"

"Maybe it can eat me!" Anna cried. "Help me!"

"Everyone tie themselves together with the bungee cords," Molly said. "Anna, we'll toss you one end and then anchor you to pull yourself out, just like if it was quicksand."

"Quicksand with the Loch Ness freaking monster in it! Hurry!"

Yoshi had been so involved with the rescue that he hadn't yet translated for the sisters. So Akiko might not have known the plan when she began walking over to Anna. She was light enough that the sand barely shifted beneath her feet, and when the team shouted at her to step back, she only waved them away, then used the same hand to offer Anna a way out.

Relieved and grateful, Anna took her hand. With that, and her right foot braced against the top of the sand, Anna was able to pry herself out.

"Thank you," Anna said.

"*Omoshiroi*," Akiko replied. Interesting.

Which, as far as Anna was concerned, was Akiko's way of saying, "You're welcome."

Molly snatched her into a hug as soon as she was clear of the area where she had sunk, and Oliver joined in from behind. Anna stood straight, her stiff arms hanging uncomfortably at her sides until it was over. Was she supposed to have hugged them back? If so, how? Molly had pinned her arms down when she grabbed her.

Akiko got the next round of hugs, although she returned

them looking far more natural than Anna had felt. Anna decided to imitate that next time, if there was a next time.

"But why did that happen?" Molly asked, checking the area around them again. "We shouldn't go forward without knowing what to watch out for."

"Maybe there's nothing to watch for," Yoshi said. "Maybe we're in some sort of messed-up TV show and they're just playing with us."

"There's a scientific reason for it," Anna said. "There's a scientific reason for everything. Every question has an answer."

"Then here's my answer on the blood sand," Yoshi said. "The sooner we get across it, the better."

Everyone agreed with that and set off at an even quicker pace straight ahead. Hercules had stopped rolling as soon as it was out of range of Javi's remote. Once they caught up with it, the machine continued bobbing along again as if nothing had happened.

That was the problem with robots. It didn't care that Anna had sunk in the sand up to one knee, or that the entire team had to stop to help her. It only knew that it was told to ride forward, and as long as it was in range, it would keep going forward until its battery ran out, until it hit a barricade, or until its programmer changed its orders.

Anna decided that Yoshi was opposite in every way. He never seemed to run out of energy. If he hit a barricade, he'd just knock it down with his sword, and he followed nobody's orders but his own.

Anna caught up to him. "Can you tell me how to say thank you in Japanese? I want to thank Akiko in her own language."

"It'd be better if Akiko learned English," Yoshi said.

"Please!" Anna said.

Yoshi smiled. "All right. Tell her, '*Watashi wa mushi o tabemasu.*'"

Anna repeated it back for him, just to be sure, and when he nodded, she ran up to Akiko and said, "*Watashi wa mushi o tabemasu.*"

Akiko looked over at Kira as if confused, then back at Anna, and when her eyes connected with Yoshi's, the three of them burst out in laughter.

"What did I say?" Anna protested. "I said it just the way you told me to!"

Yoshi was laughing so hard he was bent over with his hands braced against his thighs. Kira and Akiko had arms around each other, laughing just as hard.

"That was mean, I'm sorry," Yoshi said. "The phrase I told you means, 'I eat worms.'"

With that, the rest of Team Killbot began laughing, too, which only made Kira and Akiko laugh even harder. Kira released her sister to offer a hand of friendship to Anna, and as she did, Akiko wiped tears of laughter from her eyes.

And immediately sank to her knees.

"It's water!" Molly yelled. "That's what softens the sand. Anything moist—sweat, tears . . . blood!"

"Stop!" Yoshi said to Akiko. He'd forgotten to say it in

Japanese, but she understood. His tone was certainly unmistakable.

She nodded, but her eyes were full of fear and she was calling to her sister in Japanese. Yoshi was speaking to her, too, but Anna wasn't sure she was listening. Akiko's voice just kept raising in pitch as her panic grew. She put both hands down on the sand to try to free herself.

Both of her hands, wet with tears.

"No, don't!" Anna cried. "That'll only make it—"

Exactly where Akiko's hands went down, the sand softened again. From this angle, it was easy to see the ripples that moved outward from her hands, like a pond where a rock had been thrown.

Akiko must've felt what was happening even before Anna saw it, because she uttered a panicked cry.

And then she sank, disappearing completely beneath the sand.

Akiko was gone.

# 14

## Molly

The instant that Akiko disappeared, Molly's mind flew into action. "Everyone drop your water and follow me!" she yelled. "We've got to dig her out!"

"There's no time for that!" Javi said. "Besides, we'll sweat so much in digging, we'll all go under, too!"

"The first exposure to water only sinks you to your knees," Anna said. "If we calculate—"

"Engineers!" Yoshi shouted. "Do you want to stand there and debate, or rescue Akiko?" He began tying himself to one end of the bungee cord. "Nobody pulls me out unless I tug on this three times, got it?" He threw the end of the cord to Anna. "Now someone give me their water bottle."

Javi tossed his bottle to Yoshi, who took a deep breath, then yanked off the cap. He dumped its contents onto the sand at his feet. Before the bottle was even halfway empty, Yoshi had vanished, too, swallowed up entirely.

The remaining team all took hold of the other end of the cord, each of them waiting for the promised three tugs.

"That was one!" Oliver shouted.

"Maybe he needs more length to find Akiko," Javi said. "Let's give him some slack."

"If the creature that brushed past my leg is still down there, maybe one tug is just the creature grabbing Yoshi," Anna said.

"Stop talking like that!" Molly yelled.

"Sorry," Anna said, then her face brightened. "That was another tug!"

"Does that count as a second tug?" Oliver asked. "Or do we start counting over if the tugs don't come together?"

Just ahead of Molly, Kira had started crying. Molly let one hand go from the cord long enough to give her shoulder a squeeze, a comfort and a warning. Kira couldn't let those tears touch the sand. If she did, she'd sink, and might sink them all with her. Kira seemed to understand and wiped her eyes with her sleeve.

"The creature you felt," Molly said to Anna, "what was it like?"

"It was slick, like an eel, but something that felt like a tentacle tried to grab me. It was huge. I'm calling it a sand grabber."

"Yoshi should be out by now." Javi pulled on the cord, but nothing came in response. "How long can the guy hold his breath?"

"It's been even longer for Akiko," Oliver said.

"We're not giving up on them," Molly said. "Is anyone else sweating?"

"Yes," Anna said.

"Like a fish," Javi said.

"Well, don't sweat on me," Oliver said. "I'm dry."

"Akiko," Kira mumbled, barely getting the name out before beginning to cry again.

"We'll give him ten more seconds," Molly said. "Then I want everyone else to drop the cord and get to one of those rocks off to our left."

"What about you?" Javi asked.

Molly turned back to look at him. His forehead was glistening, and he was sporting a mustache of sweat. "Count to ten, Javi, then you run. And don't you dare let a drop of sweat fall until then."

"That was another tug!" Oliver shouted. "One!"

"Two!" Anna said.

"*San!*" Kira said.

"Pull!" Molly felt strength surge into her injured shoulder. It only took a couple of hauls before Akiko's body pushed upward through the sand. She began heaving in great gasps of air, but rolled onto her side on the sand, her whole body rising and falling with each breath.

Yoshi came up beneath her, but his body was curled into a ball and he was making no effort to take in any air.

"Is he—" Oliver started.

"He tugged on the rope!" Molly said. "He's got to be all right!"

She hoped that was true. Yoshi still wasn't moving.

With one more heave, Yoshi was pulled entirely free of the sand and lay on his side near Akiko, facing away from them.

"Yoshi!" Anna dropped the rope and ran toward him, then stopped when she got closer. "Oh, gross."

"What? What happened?" Molly rushed over to him. Out of the corner of her eye, she saw Kira and Javi attending to Akiko, who was sitting up now.

Yoshi was still on his side, panting hard, trying to catch his breath. And from Anna's reaction, Molly was expecting something terrible had happened to Yoshi's face, or maybe he was covered in sand grabber spit or . . . other fluids.

But other than being covered in sand, Yoshi looked the same as always. Anna had reacted to the thing Yoshi was holding in his arms. It was the same grayish green as the trees of this desert, but with an oily sheen on its smooth skin. It had an eel-like face, but no eyes. Of course it wouldn't need eyes. It moved through the blood sand blindly, reacting to the sound or scent of liquid.

"So that's what a sand grabber looks like," Anna said.

"Only the sand grabber's head," Yoshi said, finally getting enough breath to speak. "I killed it."

# 15

## Javi

After Akiko was back on her feet and Yoshi had recovered enough to wrap the . . . severed head into a long-sleeve shirt from his backpack, Molly ordered everyone onto the closest rocks.

It spread the group out wider than Javi wanted them to be, but at least everyone was standing on something solid, a big plus considering the alternative was being snatched up by the sand grabbers.

"Do you think that was the only one?" Javi called out to Yoshi.

"How should I know?" Yoshi replied. "I didn't hang out down there long enough to meet its friends."

"What was it like?" Anna asked.

"Ever go to the beach and let your family bury you in the sand?" Yoshi said. "Well, it was like that, except your face gets buried, too, and instead of a couple of inches, it's several feet deep, and instead of little sand crabs scuttling around beneath you, there's a monster the length of a bus and with tentacles like oily tanglevine."

"So can we agree not to hold our post-escape party on the beach?" Javi offered. Everyone laughed, but he'd been serious. Until about ten seconds ago, the beach had been one of his favorite places in the world. It had moved down a few notches on the favorites list now, below the dentist, the principal's office, and the inside of a medieval dungeon.

"We have to stick to the rocks as much as possible," Molly said. "Look for the nearest one, make sure you're totally dry, and then run for it. Don't sweat, don't cry, don't stop for a drink of water. Don't—"

"We get the theme," Yoshi said blandly.

"And if you sink to your knees, one of us will come to pull you out. Don't make it worse by touching the sand with a wet hand." Molly waited until Yoshi had translated for the sisters, and then said, "Everyone get ready, and run!"

With a sudden thrust of energy, Team Killbot burst forward, crossing the sand toward the nearest cluster of rocks. Which worked fine, until Javi realized he and Kira were headed for the same one. She reached it first, and when he hesitated on the sand, unsure of where to run next, she held out her hand, motioning for him to join her.

Javi had to put his arm around her waist to keep them both balanced on the rock. Kira smiled and said something to him in Japanese. He wished he knew the translation, but he certainly wasn't going to ask Yoshi to do it. Yoshi was still teasing him about the pink ponies shirt. He didn't need to give the guy bonus material.

So he only smiled back at Kira, and when Molly called out for them to run again, he made sure he had his eye on a rock in a different direction from where Kira was looking.

Javi was last to arrive, again. This time he and Oliver had been headed for the same rock, and although Oliver offered to let him share, Javi only shook his head and kept going. This time, he would run even farther ahead, and be the first to choose a spot.

Except he must have shaken his head too hard. His hair flicked off a bead of sweat, probably nothing more, and Javi felt one leg fall through the sand, up nearly to his thigh.

He tried not to panic, but he couldn't help wondering if there was something under the sand, reaching out for him with a slimy tendril . . .

He yelped.

"Javi, don't move. I'm coming for you." Molly was almost at his side already. She reached down and pulled him out, then said, "C'mon, let's go."

Javi ran, but almost immediately, Molly cried out. He turned. Now her leg had fallen in.

"Your hands are sweating!" she said. "Don't come back for me; you won't help. Just get to a rock."

Kira and Oliver both ran for Molly, then stopped and stared

at each other to silently determine who was the driest between them. Javi saw Oliver wipe his brow with his shirt. Kira took that as her sign to move forward and help Molly.

"This is ridiculous!" Yoshi cried from his position of one leg down in the sand. "It wasn't me! My canteen tipped over. The lid must not have been screwed on tight enough!"

"Okay, everyone who can get to a rock, go stand on one now," Molly yelled. "Javi, Oliver—rock!"

Akiko was already on a rock and not moving for anyone's rescue. She was still completely covered in red sand. Javi figured she had earned the right to stay there for as long as she wanted.

Once Molly was free, she cautiously moved toward Yoshi, checking herself the entire way for any beads of sweat. So far, so good. Kira stayed a few steps behind her. A minute later, everyone was safely back onto the rocks.

"We can't keep doing this," Yoshi said. "It's like playing leapfrog for our lives."

"That's exactly what's at stake," Molly said. "Which is why we're going to keep doing it. Everyone got your eye on a rock? Then run!"

The sun was blazing overhead by now. The running wasn't helping. The fact that no one dared take out their water bottle for a single refreshing sip only made it worse. And as they moved deeper into the desert, the rocks were spaced increasingly farther apart.

Javi felt something move beneath him, and his first instinct was to jump off his rock, but then he remembered that jumping onto blood sand was hardly a solution to his problems.

"What are you standing on?" Anna asked. "Oh!"

"I'll name it!" Javi quickly called, though he wasn't yet sure what "it" was. He leaned over to look at his rock. "Hey, it's a shell!"

"It's a tortoise!" Oliver said. "A rock tortoise."

"Rock tortoise!" Anna repeated. "I like it."

Javi only folded his arms, pouting as the rock tortoise slowly carried him forward. He'd discovered it, but Oliver was getting credit for the name, such as it was. It wasn't even that creative.

"As slow as that thing moves, it'll take you weeks longer than the rest of us to cross this blood sand," Yoshi said as he ran past Javi.

"Yes, but I will definitely get across it," Javi said with a smile back. He lifted his face to the sun and enjoyed the ride.

# 16

## Molly

The group had been leapfrogging for almost a mile, Molly figured. They needed a break to cool down, catch their breath, and hopefully, to dry off. Between Kira, who was farthest ahead, and Javi, who was a long way behind them still traveling on his rock tortoise, the group was too spread out. She needed to pull them all together again, safely.

They could bungee-cord tie themselves together, so that if one went down, the others could more easily pull that person up again, but if a sand grabber got one of them, it might pull everyone else on the cord down with them. A good team either swims or sinks together, she thought, but that was only a good thing if the sinking was not literal.

In a couple of hours, the sun would be lower in the sky and

things would start to cool off. Sweat wouldn't be a problem, then. That was good news. Aside from the problem with sinking, they were probably losing too much water by running constantly. She knew how thirsty she was, how the sand was a constant grit inside her mouth, swelling her tongue and scratching her throat. Her shoulder stung a little, too. She wanted to pull back her shirt and look at it, but the rest of the group would notice. They would worry.

It wasn't their job to worry. Molly was the leader. She would do the worrying for all of them.

That was always how things were for her.

Before Molly's father had died, he was the designated family worrier. He worried about getting everyone to school or work on time, about paying each month's bills, about Molly getting top scores on her homework.

After his death, someone had to take on that job. Molly's mother didn't worry, or cry, or even get angry. Since his death, Molly's mother had stopped feeling anything at all. Her days were spent wandering in a fog of silence, just doing the routines, looking at nothing, seeing nothing around her.

So Molly took over. She got herself to school and made sure her mother went to work with some kind of breakfast in her hand. She paid the bills and told her mother how much money they had left for groceries each week. And Molly wasn't necessarily worried about getting top scores on her homework—she knew how smart she was, knew she had the potential to become anything she wanted to be. She only worried that it wouldn't be good enough to pull her mother out of her emptiness.

Here, in the rift, Molly was the leader again. Which meant there was no time to think about her mom or her shoulder or anything else but getting her team across the blood sand.

"We're going to rest for a while," she called out. "You should be fine to take a drink of water, as long as both feet are on a rock. Cool down, any way you can."

It took some time before Javi's rock tortoise finally caught up with them. He no longer had a drop of sweat on him. "I'll just go on ahead and look for Hercules," he casually said as he passed Molly. "I figure in another half hour, I'll be so far ahead that it'll take you guys at least two minutes to catch me."

At least he looked cooled off, Molly thought with a wry smile.

Javi's family seemed nearly perfect to her. It was a big family, always with room for one more. Whenever things got too quiet at her house, she'd go over to Javi's. He had probably meant it when he said Yoshi could come and live with him. And no matter how grumpy Yoshi was before setting foot in Javi's home, by the time he left, he'd have eaten enough good food to keep him full until the new year, and would have a smile on his face to last twice that long.

Yoshi was on the rock closest to her. He'd unwrapped the

sand grabber head and was looking at it. That really was disgusting.

"Why did you wrap it?" Molly asked him.

Yoshi shrugged at her without looking back. "It's got oily skin. I think that's how it moves through the sand so easily. So if I drag it along behind me, I figure I'm just asking to sink."

"And you haven't had any problems with it all wrapped up?" Molly asked.

"Obviously not."

An idea had sparked in Molly's head. She unzipped her backpack and pulled out the two emergency blankets from the pilots' box. She unfolded the first, about as wide as a lap quilt. It was like a thin sheet of foil, but strong enough to resist being torn. She laid it wide on the sand, then stepped onto it. The foil reflected the sunlight, casting a glare onto her eyes, but she looked away, and then unfolded the second, tossing it a little ahead of her. Once she was on the second, she pulled up the first and put that one ahead.

This was a new game of leapfrog. The emergency blankets would catch any moisture that happened to fall. And there was enough room on each blanket for everyone to stand. It would be slower than running, but cost them less energy.

She offered a hand to Yoshi to help him onto the blanket, but he only blinked back at her with a blank expression. "I'd rather run for it."

"Well, it's not your choice, Yoshi, because I can't risk losing you."

"Lead the team if you want, but I think I've already made it clear that you're not my boss."

"I know. But I can ask for your help, right?" Molly watched the change in his expression when she said that, and added, "We wouldn't have gotten out of that jungle without you, Akiko wouldn't have gotten away from the sand grabber without you, and I'm convinced we'll need your help all the way to that structure ahead. I don't know what the problem is with your family back home, but here in the rift, *we* are your family and we need you alive. Please help me."

Yoshi stared back at her, and for a moment, she wasn't sure if he would cooperate. But he gave a half smile and jumped onto the blanket, holding out his hand for the second one, which he tossed ahead of them. They leapfrogged to pick up Anna and Akiko next, then Oliver, and Kira last.

This definitely was slower than the runs had been, but since it was so hot, nobody was complaining. And when they did need to rest, it was easy to settle down on the blankets, or even lie on them, not too different from a beach blanket.

Finally, they made enough progress to see Javi in the distance. He wasn't on his rock tortoise anymore. He was on the sand, standing perfectly still.

"Are you okay?" Oliver called.

Javi motioned for them to come forward. The blankets

were tossed one in front of the other more quickly now, until they had settled in about twenty feet behind Javi.

"Do you see that? he asked.

Molly squinted across the sand. "I don't see anything."

Javi turned around to smile at them. "Exactly," he said. Then he took a step forward and vanished from view.

# 17

## Yoshi

J avi was gone.

Vanished.

*Kiemashita.*

"Javi!" Molly sprang forward before Yoshi pulled her back.

"Don't," he said. "Not until we figure out where he went."

The rest of the Killbots were agitated, too. "He might've sank into the sand, like Akiko," Anna offered.

"She said my name," Akiko told Yoshi. "What did she say?"

"Not now," Yoshi growled in Japanese.

"It could be a portal," Oliver said. "Transporting him from one place to another, maybe even out of the rift."

"None of us knows where he is," Anna said. "It does no good to make guesses. We have to look at the evidence and then come up with logical conclusions."

"Javi!" Kira cried.

"Yes, we know," Yoshi told her, rolling his eyes. "Javi's gone."

"No," she said, pointing. "He's not."

Yoshi followed her gaze. Javi was standing right where he'd been a moment ago, smiling a ridiculous smile.

"Did that work?" Javi asked. "I'm guessing it worked."

"What did you . . . What was that?" asked Oliver.

"Check it out," Javi said. He took a step backward, disappearing again. Then he rematerialized as he stepped forward. "Is it cool?" he asked.

Yoshi didn't admit it out loud, but it was pretty cool.

Molly's jaw had dropped. "Did you find a . . . What is even the word for that?"

"A cloaking field," Yoshi offered, and Molly and Oliver gave him a surprised look. "What?" he said. "I read manga."

"I would have gone right past it, but I saw Hercules disappear and then come out the other end," Javi explained. "And there's something in there—something you can only see from inside the field. Like a big metal cylinder."

"Theories?" Molly prodded.

"Is it the source of the field?" Anna asked. "A new device?"

"Or it's what the field was created to hide," Oliver said.

"Maybe," Javi said. "But it looks like it opens. I'm going to take a peek inside."

"Wait," Molly said. "That might not be a great idea."

"Unless it turns out to be precisely that: a great idea," Javi said. "It's like a big metal cabinet with rounded ends. It could have food in it, or medicine. Maybe it's some super satellite phone with a direct line to the people who are looking for us."

"Or it could contain something that will try to kill you," Anna said with a shrug. "It could be anything."

"What are they saying to each other?" Kira asked for maybe the hundredth time that day.

"I thought you were going to learn English," Yoshi answered.

"Maybe they can learn a little Japanese, too," Kira retorted.

Yoshi sighed and caught her and Akiko up on the conversation, then added, "Molly had a bad dream last night, and I think it's got her spooked. She thinks Javi and Oliver are the only ones who know about it."

"Oliver reminds me of our brother," Akiko said. Yoshi hadn't realized they had a brother. He wondered about him, for some reason. He would've liked to have a brother, too, someone to whack him on the arm when he was acting stupid.

"What are they saying about me?" Oliver asked. He was looking over at them, having recognized his name.

"They think you're cute," Yoshi said, enjoying the sight of Oliver blushing and knowing the sisters wouldn't understand why. "One of them has a crush on you."

"Oh, uh, which one?" Oliver asked, looking genuinely afraid. The kid obviously had no experience with crushes.

Before Yoshi could make up an answer, Javi said, "I'm going to check it out. I think we have to take the risk that something in it will help us."

"Okay, but tie yourself to the rope," Molly said, tossing one end over to him. "If something happens, I want an easy way to pull you back to us."

Javi picked up his end of the rope and tied it around his waist. His smile and wide eyes revealed his excitement to test out the object, which made Yoshi even more nervous.

"Be careful!" Oliver called. Yoshi noticed he looked over at the sisters when he said that, still wondering which of the girls had the crush on him.

When Javi had finished knotting the rope, he wiped both hands down his pants, then tiptoed forward across the sand.

"Are you sweating?" Anna called.

"Even a little?" Molly asked. "It only takes one drop."

"Now I'm starting to sweat, thanks to you two," Javi said. "Just let me do this and stop fussing!"

"No *mizu*, Javi," Kira said in broken English. Javi must've figured out that she was reminding him about water, too. But she wouldn't know why he turned around to roll his eyes at her before he disappeared.

The rope was visible to the edge of the field, then vanished just as Javi had. It was a strange sight, as if the rope were floating on its own, moving and bobbing gently with Javi's invisible movements.

Oliver giggled. "Javi, it looks like you're dancing!" he said.

Javi seemed to take this as encouragement. The rope moved more dramatically, swaying back and forth and then jiggling. Yoshi couldn't figure out what Javi might be doing to make it move that way. Suddenly, the pink ponies shirt reappeared out of nowhere and landed on the blood sand. He must've taken it off and tossed it. Being moist with sweat, the shirt immediately sank into the depths of the sand. Yoshi figured Javi would be okay with that.

"We can understand ditching the shirt, but if you toss out any other clothing, we're going to ask you to stay invisible," Yoshi teased.

Javi's laughter rang out as the rope shook. It was a little disconcerting.

Javi seemed to get back to business after that. The rope went taut as he apparently moved toward the cylindrical object. There was a long moment of stillness and silence.

And then Javi's bloodcurdling scream rang out across the desert.

"Pull him back!" Akiko said.

"Go help him!" said Kira.

"Quiet!" Yoshi said. He drew his sword, while Molly and the others pulled hard on the rope. Javi lurched back into view, falling back onto the sand and slipping partway beneath the surface. He wasn't moving.

"I'll get him," Yoshi said. "The rest of you, stay put!"

Yoshi kept his sword at the ready. He didn't like that Javi was lying on the ground, seemingly indifferent to the fact that he was one sweat droplet away from being a sand grabber's lunch. What had happened to him?

"Javi? Are you stuck?" Yoshi realized he was speaking to him like he was a four-year-old kid who had just dropped his ice-cream cone. "I'm coming to get you."

Javi didn't answer. But with his free hand, he wiped at his eyes and sniffed hard.

"Javi, give me your hand so I can pull you out."

"Can you see me now?" Javi asked.

"Yeah. I can see you're halfway submerged in blood sand. Give me your hand."

With Yoshi's help, Javi pulled himself out of the sand. Molly was calling to them to hurry back onto the emergency blankets. But not yet, Yoshi decided. Javi didn't look too steady.

Javi's eyes darted around. "Where's my shirt? I guess pink ponies are better than a desert sunburn."

Yoshi half smiled. "It's sand grabber food now." Javi's shoulders slumped and he stuffed his fists into the shreds of his pocket, looking as if losing his pink ponies shirt was somehow the worst news he'd ever heard. Before he could say anything, Yoshi took off his backpack, unzipped it, and pulled out one of the shirts that he had salvaged from his own luggage the night before. "This will probably fit."

Javi held it up, a short-sleeve button-up with black shoulders and a checkerboard torso. A very cool shirt as far as Yoshi was concerned. "You sure you want to give this to me?" Javi asked. "If you were lucky enough to find the one piece of luggage with clothes that look like your style, then—" He stopped, realization dawning in his eyes. "Oh. That was your bag, wasn't it?" He paused again. "That's why you've been so upset." He started to put on the shirt. "I won't tell the others. And maybe you won't tell them why I sank into the sand? About the crying?"

Yoshi clamped a hand over Javi's shoulder and started to lead him back toward the blankets. "All I could see is that you were sweating, dude. Just like the rest of us."

# 18

## Javi

Oliver punched Javi lightly on the arm. "That was so cool! Did you know you were invisible before we told you? What made you reappear again? Did the desert look different while you were invisible? Could you see us?"

"Yeah, it was . . . pretty cool," Javi said. His mind was somewhere else entirely.

"What did you see?" Molly asked.

Javi took a deep breath. "I saw some bones. Old, bleached bones in a metal container. I guess it startled me."

That was true enough, Javi figured. He just hoped nobody asked for more details.

Molly looked skeptical, and Anna said, "That was quite a scream."

"Like I said, I was startled," Javi insisted. "I was hoping for pizza and found bones." He tried a smile.

"While you and Yoshi were talking, I made some calculations," Oliver said. "I estimated the distance based on what Yoshi described seeing from the top of the hill, the ratio of the desert to the overall hologram map that Anna saw in the cave, and how far we've traveled already. If we leapfrog the way we've been doing, we won't get off this sand until sometime tomorrow."

"What if we run?" Anna asked. "Then we would have a shot at getting off tonight. We could make camp on better ground."

"Where we can find water, and hopefully some food," Yoshi said. "And I don't know if any of you drool in your sleep, but let's not find out while we're still on the sand. It's a no-brainer. We should run."

"If we run, someone else will go down in the sand," Javi said. "I think sweat is a bigger risk than drooling."

"Every minute we're on the sand, our risk of someone going down increases!" Yoshi turned to Oliver. "Calculate those odds!"

"It's cooled off a lot," Molly said. "We shouldn't have as much of a problem with sweating. But running directly on the sand does pose a greater risk. Let's take a vote."

Yoshi translated for the sisters, and reported that both agreed with him, though Javi wasn't sure that was true. Kira was a risk-taker, but Akiko was still standing in the very center of her emergency blanket. No way had she voted to run.

"I vote for safety," Oliver said. "It only costs us a day to continue leapfrogging."

"But if it's another day like we've already had, I want off this sand," Anna said. "I think we should run."

"Leapfrog," Javi said. He needed to slow down, to think about the implications of what he'd seen. Rushing anywhere right now seemed like a bad idea.

"Sorry, Javi," Molly said. "I'm voting to run. Even with the blankets, we're safer if we can sleep on solid ground tonight."

Assuming that whatever came after the blood sand was safer. Everyone wanted to believe that was true, but there was no way to know for sure. He didn't say it out loud, though.

Molly made everyone double-check their water containers to be sure nothing was leaking. Everyone claimed to be dry again, and the first breeze of the *yokaze* gave them hope that if someone did start to sweat, the night wind would solve that problem. When they were sure it was safe, Molly folded up the emergency blankets and returned them to her backpack.

Yoshi had his sword sheathed, but his hand was on its hilt, ready to pull it out if necessary. Javi stuck his hand inside his pocket, the knife tight in his grip.

"We run together," Molly said. "No one gets too far ahead, and absolutely no one gets left behind. If you run into trouble, holler for help and the closest person will help you get out." She waited for Yoshi to finish translating, then said, "We run for four minutes, rest for one minute. Everyone ready? Go!"

The team left at exactly the same time and did as Molly

had instructed. Akiko was a slower runner, but Kira was right at her side, holding her hand and pulling her along. Yoshi was fast, but kept an eye out for Oliver behind him. Anna, Javi, and Molly made up the last of the group, though they were almost on the heels of the rest of their team.

When about four minutes had passed, Molly called for everyone to stop and rest. Javi was glad to catch his breath, but was also surprised to discover that he preferred the run. When he ran, he had to focus on the team, on keeping himself dry, and on anything happening around them.

Here, when he was still, he had time to think about what he'd seen in the cloaking field.

"Javi," Akiko whispered beside him. When he looked over, she smiled and gave him a thumbs-up, which spoke more than her few words of English allowed her.

He nodded back, reminding himself that this blood sand was their current problem, and everything else had to wait for now.

"Go!" Molly said.

They ran again, passing a whole spine of rocks that Javi was sure Molly must have seen. She didn't order them onto the rocks, though. She just wanted them going forward as fast as possible. So he redoubled his efforts, imagining there was something snapping at his heels. It was all too easy to picture, and it kept him moving.

"And stop," Molly said four minutes later. She looked back. "I think we've come a long way. Maybe almost a mile."

"Recalculating," Oliver said. Seconds later, he nodded. "I think we can do this."

"That's not very specific for someone's who supposed to be good at math," Yoshi said. "What were you recalculating, exactly?"

"Our odds," Oliver said. "I didn't figure you'd want the exact number, but since you asked, back where we started our run, our odds of getting off of the blood sand were about a hundred to one. Now they're . . . better."

"Enough talk," Molly said. "Everyone get ready, and run!"

And so they did, starting and stopping and starting again, continuing forward in fast-paced bursts of dry sprints for what seemed like an hour. Javi's mouth had become its own desert, his tongue sticking mercilessly to the roof of his mouth, and he was sure everyone else felt the same way, but nobody suggested bringing out their water. His legs were beginning to ache, and even after a minute's rest, he couldn't catch enough of a breath to begin running with nearly as much energy as before.

There was some good news. He'd finally gotten Hercules in range again and pushed the remote control to stop his rolling. When they had caught up with it, Javi picked up the robot and inspected it.

"I agree, it's been useless in protecting us," Javi said, "but at least it hasn't tripped over its whiskers."

"Not yet," Yoshi said.

"Let's just walk for a while," Molly said, although Javi could tell she wasn't nearly as winded as he was. "At least we're moving forward."

"Good," Anna said. "Because I have some questions for Javi."

Javi groaned. He just wanted to get Hercules strapped onto his back and think about nothing more complicated than that. "Later, okay?"

"These are important now. For instance, how do we know there isn't a cloaking field beside us right here?"

That was a fair question, and luckily, one he could answer without getting a pit in his stomach. "I didn't see the cloaking field at first, but once I knew it was there, I could see that the light was distorted around it. Not much, maybe how it would look if you were wearing a pair of glasses with a prescription that was a little off. Trust me, this whole run I've been watching everything around us. There's no distortions."

"But if we did see a distortion, what does that mean?" Oliver asked. "Is it a buried device like the ones we found in the jungle? Do *our* devices have a stealth setting?"

"I'm more concerned about the possibility of an ambush we can't see coming," Yoshi said.

Javi shrugged. "I think even if there's another cloaking field, it's probably empty. Nothing was in the first one."

"Just a pile of bones in a metal cabinet?" Anna asked.

"Uh, yeah," Javi said.

Anna stepped closer to him. If she noticed the beads of sweat forming on his forehead or his increased rate of breathing, she didn't care. "Were they human bones?" she asked.

"No, and I don't want to—"

"An animal?"

"I—I don't know."

"How could you not know?"

"Enough, Anna!" Molly said. "He's not ready—"

Javi stopped and turned to face Anna directly. He knew he was going to yell, but he didn't care anymore. "What I saw was a monster. It was hideous, like a human skeleton but . . . tall, and angular. It was misshapen and covered in slime and . . . and it didn't look like anything I've ever seen. And if it had been alive, I'm pretty sure it would have shredded me to bits in an instant. Are you happy now? Does that answer your questions?"

"Sort of." Anna paused, as if trying to think of something to say. Finally, she said, "I'm sorry, Javi. I can understand why that would be unsettling."

Javi almost laughed. "*Unsettling*," he said. "Sure. That's one word for it."

But it was hard to put into words just how spooked he was. That skeleton had looked real to him, which meant it had once belonged to a living, breathing creature.

And that led directly to the question that guaranteed he'd be having nightmares for as long as they were stuck here.

Were they sharing the rift with a living version of that thing?

## Anna

She had pushed too far, again. As she always took everything too far. Deep inside, Anna had always wondered if the only reason Team Killbot allowed her to work with them was because of her talent with robotics, and not because they liked her. She knew she wasn't the easiest person to like.

This time, she planned to make it up to Javi. Of everyone in their group, she had the best chance to understand the biology of the rift. All living things—even "monsters"—had strengths and weaknesses. If there were creatures out there that frightened Javi, she could figure out their weaknesses, and then they could defeat anything that threatened them. It was simple science.

Molly had the team running again. She said she'd spotted trees up ahead, which Anna couldn't see yet, but she didn't say anything about it possibly being a mirage. Even if Anna was right, Molly would take offense at the suggestion that the trees were only a figment of her dehydrated imagination. Maybe Molly had better eyes. The landscape did seem different on the horizon.

Anna was pleased with herself for keeping that entire train of thought in her own head. Not that she had much breath for speaking.

After another few bursts forward, Yoshi gave a whoop of joy and ran even faster. She looked to where he was pointing and realized Molly had been right—those were trees ahead. They were still only desert trees, but had a few actual leaves. Leaves meant water.

Kira said something to Yoshi, who translated, "The sisters want to keep running until we're off the blood sand. I agree!"

Team Killbot cheered. Everyone saw the trees by now, not far from some tall rocks right at the edge of the blood sand.

Tall . . . identically shaped rocks. That wasn't possible.

Anna stopped running. Akiko was closest to her, so Anna grabbed her hand. The rest of Team Killbot stopped moments later, seeing the same problem she had already noticed.

"Pincer robots," Yoshi muttered. "Five of them."

They were spaced out along the edge of the blood sand, each one facing the team and with their pincers raised. The only way off the sand was to get past them.

"What do we do?" Oliver asked, stepping toward Yoshi.

Javi grabbed Hercules from off his back and turned on the

battery again. "We can use this as a distraction. Send it off to the right while we remain still, and hope the pincer robots follow it." He looked at the robot as he set it on the ground. "Sorry, Hercules."

Anna remembered the joke Yoshi had made about Javi kissing Hercules good-bye. Javi looked so sad now, she almost thought he might do it.

To her surprise, Anna realized she felt a desire to say good-bye to the robot, too. They had built Hercules from scratch, from nothing more than metal parts scattered across a table. She was proud of the job her team had done. They had all hoped Hercules would win that competition—that it would come through for them, follow their instructions, and take down the competition.

And she supposed, they felt the same hopes for Hercules now. It was only the stakes that were different. Hercules had to be sacrificed in order to defend the team. Even though it was only a robot, the thought of losing it made her feel sad, too.

Anna wasn't sure how to deal with that. Emotions were hard.

She knelt beside Javi, put a hand on Hercules, and said, "Thanks, little toaster. Win this one for our team, okay?"

Anna and Javi released Hercules, who rolled to the right, his soccer-kicking appendage ready for battle.

Sensing the movement, the pincers responded, aiming their attention toward Hercules.

"Now what?" Oliver asked.

Anna pulled out the device she had been carrying in her backpack. "What about using low tech? It exploded the mites."

"These things are five times the size," Javi said. "That's five times the explosion. Five times the amount of metal scrap in the air."

"Then let's use low gravity," Anna said. "Stir up some sand twisters."

Molly's grin was cautious. "That's a risk to us, too."

"We can dodge the twisters," Javi said. "Not explosions."

Molly pulled out her device as well. "Okay, but let's make a run for it, getting as close to the edge of the blood sand as we can. As soon as the robots are within range, or if they cut us off, turn on the low grav and hope it works like before."

Yoshi had been translating, and everyone heard Kira's loud sigh. He turned to the rest of the team and said, "She thinks this is a terrible plan."

"A terrible plan is better than no plan," Javi said.

Was it? Anna wondered. Chaos certainly had its place in nature. Regardless, she rotated the disk to the "low tech" setting, but she'd use it only as a last resort.

"Everyone ready?" Molly asked. "We'll all stay together. Now . . . run!"

Team Killbot ran leftward in a tight cluster, loosely aiming for the trees they had spotted earlier. Anna happened to look up and notice the green moon had just peeked over the horizon.

"*Midori*," Kira said, pointing out the same moon to the rest of the group.

*Midori.* Go ahead and die if you ignore it.

The pincer robots had noticed they were running and changed direction. Javi slowed long enough to raise his remote control and adjust Hercules's bearing to intercept the robots. It got right in front of one, which Anna hoped would force it to slow down. Instead, it only lowered one pincer and snapped Hercules in half, then continued rolling toward them as if Hercules had been nothing more than a sheet of tinfoil.

Javi grimaced. "They're coming," he called over to Anna. "Is the disk ready?"

Anna nodded, but she still hoped to outrun them. If they turned on the devices now, a column could erupt right beneath their feet.

"Faster, Oliver!" Molly cried. "Keep up with me!"

Oliver lowered his head and tried to give an extra burst of speed, but Anna saw how hard he was breathing. The team would have to slow down or they'd leave him behind. Neither was acceptable.

The closest robot was very close to them now. Its pincers were raised and widening as it bore down on Akiko.

"I'm turning on my device!" Molly called.

"Me too!" Anna even aimed it toward the robots, in case it made a difference.

With a huge swooshing sound, the first column of sand shot up between her and Molly, cutting them off from each other. Anna felt a bounce in her step now as gravity lessened, and she used that to widen the stride in her run. Somewhere nearby, she heard Molly shouting orders, but the swirling sand kept her from hearing the words. Another column rose between Kira and Akiko, separating them. "Keep running!" she cried at the sisters, knowing it was a useless thing to say.

"We got one!" Javi pointed up to a column that must have arisen beneath one of the robots. It was caught up in the swirling mass, rising higher and higher into the air. Its pincers snapped wildly, trying to find anything to grasp on to.

Yoshi suddenly ran into view with Kira at his side. He had one end of their rope in his hands and Kira had the other. Together, they ran past the nearest robot, crossed the rope behind it, and ran forward again, tightening the rope. They tried digging their heels into the sand, forcing the robot off balance, but they were outside the bounds of the low-gravity fields, and the robot was too heavy.

Javi joined them, sneaking up behind the robot to pull at the rope where it crossed together. He yanked on it, but it still wasn't enough.

Oliver ran over next. He stopped beside Javi, then hit the robot with a rock he must've found in the sand. It didn't make a dent in the metal, but it did get the robot's attention. It stopped pursuing Akiko and tried rotating its body around. Yoshi and Kira tightened the rope again, and this time the robot's own movement threw off its balance, and it fell forward. It flailed about in the sand, too top-heavy to regain its footing.

"Let's take down the next one!" Yoshi yelled.

"We just have to run!" Molly cried. "It's too chaotic out here!" Over a dozen columns of swirling sand had already risen, and more were appearing each minute.

Yoshi wasn't giving up so easily. He pulled out his canteen, unscrewed the lid, and threw the rest of his water beneath two of the three remaining robots. They immediately sank into the sand.

In their rippling wake, Anna saw the thrashing of a sand grabber's tail.

That was bad news. If they kept throwing water around, they risked sinking themselves, and that sand grabber would be waiting.

"Oliver, look out!" Yoshi yelled.

It had happened so fast, Anna could scarcely believe it. The last remaining robot had Oliver in its pincers. All it had to do was squeeze.

"No!" Molly cried.

Yoshi withdrew his sword, and Kira pulled out her water.

"No water!" Molly ordered. She waved a hand to get Kira's attention. "No! You understand? Oliver will go under, too!"

The robot began dragging Oliver backward, deeper onto the blood sand. Team Killbot cautiously followed.

"What do we do?" Anna looked over to Molly for an answer, and it was clear Molly didn't know.

For his part, Oliver looked terrified. His eyes were wide, but he knew better than to cry—he knew the awful consequences of those tears dropping onto the sand as well as anyone.

"Low tech," Yoshi said. "Just weaken it enough that I can fight it. Dial down the device a little bit."

Anna shook her head at Molly. If there was any setting on the device between full on and off, she didn't know it, and now wasn't the time to experiment.

The robot was moving faster now, taking Oliver with it. "Help me!" he cried.

"Options," Molly said to her team. "I need more options!"

They didn't have any options. None. Anna wasn't being cold to think this way; it was just a fact. Anything that stopped the robot would hurt Oliver, too.

And then the decision was taken out of their hands.

Mites rose from the ground, dozens of them letting the blood sand roll off their backs. They swarmed the pincer robot en masse with their whiskers extended, coiling them around the robot's legs until it couldn't move forward. Others wrapped their whiskers around the pincers, forcing them apart until Oliver was able to slide safely to the ground.

He smiled, taking a step away from the struggle and toward his friends. But the look of joy and relief on his face flickered and was replaced with confusion. Fear.

Pain.

Anna saw the problem just as Oliver seemed to figure it out

himself. The pincer had injured him. He was bleeding through his shirt.

Bleeding onto the sand.

Oliver sank up to his waist. They all lunged forward to help him, but too late. There was a flash of movement as an oily green tendril wrapped around his body and pulled.

Before he could make a sound, Oliver had disappeared beneath the sand.

# 20

## Yoshi

**Y**oshi still had his end of the rope, and Kira still had hers. He tied it around his waist, then turned to Anna. "Give me your water!"

She did, and Yoshi dumped it over himself, feeling his body immediately sink into the sand.

He was blind down here, though he wasn't helpless. The sand grabber left behind an oily trail that made it easy to follow. As long as he stuck to the oily path, the sand was like what he imagined it would be to swim through syrup.

Which was harder than Team Killbot probably imagined. Yoshi was strong but had never considered himself athletic. If he ran, it was usually to get home before his mother realized he'd been out after curfew. Once, he'd had to outrun a mall security guard. That was it.

Saving Akiko had been relatively easy before. The sand

grabber hadn't gone far with her, and once he severed one tentacle, killing the rest of it wasn't too difficult.

But the sand grabber who took Oliver was moving fast, and Yoshi was already tired from those bursts of speed across the blood sand. The desperate need to breathe was slowing him more than before.

He found the oily trail again and swam forward through the sand, then realized he wasn't alone. Sand mites were down here, too. He could feel them zooming past him as if completely indifferent to the need for air and the difficulty of being in sand. What had Javi called this?

Friction.

The sand mites weren't slowed by the friction of the sand, not like him.

Yoshi followed in the same direction as the robots, until his lungs were about to burst. Finally, he had to push to the surface for air. He came up, startlingly close to the edge of a swirling column of sand. He knew the team couldn't normalize the gravity now, not while everyone was still on the sand, but he cursed at the realization they'd created a new hazard in defeating those robots.

Without another thought, Yoshi drew in a new breath, but by the time he got under, the oily trail had disappeared. He searched, digging deeper and deeper, but the sand grew dry and dense and resisted his every movement. His muscles ached and his lungs burned, screaming at him to surface.

When he finally heaved himself out of the sand, he lay on his side, drawing in massive gulps of air. Far behind him, he heard the cheers of Team Killbot, calling his name and shouting for joy. He wished they wouldn't.

When Yoshi remained still, the team began to realize, one by one, that something was wrong.

"Where is he?" Molly cried, running over to him. "Yoshi, where is Oliver?"

"I'm going back down," he said, his voice now hoarse and cracking. "Water!"

"You're too tired," Anna said. "Let's send someone else down."

"Give me the water," Javi offered. "I'll do it!"

"No," Molly said. "There are too many twisters now. Within a couple of minutes, they'll overtake this whole area. They'll get us, too."

Yoshi pulled himself to his feet and turned, though he couldn't look at the others. No scolding from his father had ever created the shame he felt right now.

"Where's Oliver?" Kira cried. "Yoshi, how could you lose him?"

Yoshi glared at her. He had done his best, but it wasn't good enough. Everyone had counted on him, and he had failed.

"I can try again," he insisted. "I'm going to try."

"It's been too long," Molly said, clearly fighting back tears.

Yoshi started to protest, but Javi put a hand on his shoulder, and he came up short.

Behind him, Akiko said, "You tried. We know you tried."

As much as Yoshi didn't want to hear the criticism for failing to recover Oliver, the sympathy was worse. He replaced his sword and turned away from the team, looking out across the desert. The light was quickly fading. They needed to get off the blood sand and find a place to camp.

Find a place to mourn.

Yoshi had never felt worse in his life.

Javi tugged at him. "Let's go," he said quietly. After a long moment of silence, Yoshi gave in. They turned, heads down, and began walking in silence. No one had the strength to do anything more than put one foot in front of the other, each shuffling footfall taking them another step closer to the edge of the blood sand.

One step farther from Oliver.

They passed another series of boulders, the first real sign that solid ground was nearby. "Everyone get behind the rocks," Molly said. "Let's normalize the gravity again."

The team did, though everyone leaned against the boulders, exhausted, while Molly and Anna turned off the devices. Yoshi heard the massive swoosh of collapsing sand, felt it rush against the far side of his boulder, but only closed his eyes while it happened. While everything went quiet.

Then, in the silence, the universe whispered to him. There was a sound, far off in the distance, carried on the winds across the desert sands.

It was a distant cry for help.

Yoshi wasn't the only one who'd heard it. Molly stood up straight and held up a hand for the rest of the team to remain silent.

Yoshi found a grip on the boulder, intending to climb it, but Javi grabbed his arm, pulling him down again. "Stop, Yoshi," he said sadly. "It's not Oliver." He pointed upward, where green-feathered birds were circling overhead. "It's the birds. They imitate us."

But Yoshi shook his head. He pulled free of Javi's grip and quickly scaled the rock. It put him high enough to get a good view of the blood sand, although in the low light of the red moon, the sand was cast in deep maroon. He strained his eyes to see as far as possible.

There was movement out there, but it could be anything. Mites. Sand grabbers. The *yokaze*, which was already picking up for the evening, blowing grit against his face.

"I thought I heard him," Yoshi said.

"You heard a bird that's trying to lure you in and bite you," Javi said. His voice broke. "This place is cruel like that."

"We're in no state for this," Kira said. She had her arm around Akiko, who had covered her face with her hands. "Half of us are crying. All of us are sweating. Your hair is still damp from the water you poured on yourself. It's a wonder we haven't all gone under the sand."

"You're right," he told her in Japanese. Then he told the others, "We have to get off the sand while we still can."

Everyone looked to Molly, and more than ever before,

Yoshi was glad not to be the leader. Because she was in an impossible position. Anything she said now would be wrong.

Molly's eyes were tearing up, and despite the risk of crying on blood sand, she didn't look like she could stop herself.

"We should vote," Javi said.

"No," Molly said. "I don't want to make anyone else responsible for this decision. We're getting off the sand."

Everyone erupted with an opinion, except for Yoshi. He only stared at Molly, watching her take her team's complaints like body blows.

"The sand grabber pulled Oliver under," Molly said. "It wouldn't bring him up again. Whatever we just heard, it wasn't Oliver. He's . . . Oliver is . . ."

"Oliver is dead," Yoshi said. He said it so that she wouldn't have to.

He could do that much for her, at least.

# 21

## Molly

Molly was the last of them to leave the blood sand, and stepping off it onto solid desert ground was one of the hardest things she'd ever done. It felt to her like staring Oliver in the face and saying she intended to abandon him.

Which was exactly what she had done, she supposed.

Based on the way her remaining teammates looked at her, she figured they were thinking the same thing. None of them had said a word to her for the entire trek off the blood sand. Akiko was crying, Kira's arm around her in a vain attempt at comfort. Before they decided to leave the blood sand, Yoshi had seemed to agree with Molly, but he had kept his thoughts to himself since then. Anna trailed a half step behind him, stony and silent. And Javi, who always defended Molly, had looked back about a thousand times since they left, just in case Oliver might somehow have appeared behind them.

He hadn't.

He wouldn't.

They made camp near the small grove of trees not far from the edge of the sand. Anna immediately set to work finding water. Javi asked Yoshi for the rope so he could build a shelter.

"What good is a rope gonna do?" Yoshi snarled.

"I don't know," Javi said.

Yoshi tossed it at him. "I'm going to look for food. I'm starving."

Molly had food in her backpack, and she intended to share it once everyone got settled down. But she wasn't sure everyone *would* settle down tonight. The only word to describe her team right now was *brittle*. The slightest jostle could break them all apart.

Yoshi stormed off, and this time Anna went in a different direction in her search for water. Kira and Akiko gestured to Javi that they would help him with a shelter.

Nobody asked Molly to do anything, or for her opinion on anything. Nobody was even looking at Molly. She might as well have turned invisible.

Rather than sit and sulk, which was what she felt like doing, Molly gathered some fallen branches from beneath the trees. There wasn't much for kindling, but she had all those lawyer's papers in her backpack. She liked the idea of burning some of them to lessen the weight she was carrying. When she'd gathered what they had in the area, she wandered a little farther from camp, hoping to find more wood, or to find anything to cheer up her team. Anything at all.

Once she was out of sight from the group, Molly lifted her shirtsleeve enough to inspect the injury to her shoulder. It wasn't glowing anymore, thankfully, but it wasn't getting better, either. A green rash was beginning to form on the skin, worse where it was closest to the bite. It didn't itch, but that actually bothered Molly more than if it did. A rash that itched would be like a giant mosquito bite, or a heat rash, a problem that usually went away if you ignored it. This didn't seem like that kind of a rash, nor was it showing any signs of going away. If anything, it was spreading.

She stared at the horizon, feeling hollow inside, except when torturous doubts flared in her stomach.

The red moon was above. *Aka*—that was the color. Molly liked the idea of using the Japanese words as names for the moons, to give them a way to connect with Kira and Akiko through language. It was difficult to think of everyone as one team when two of the members understood almost nothing of what was being said. Yoshi did a good job of translating most of the time, but she knew for a fact that he didn't tell them everything, and she suspected he sometimes even deliberately mistranslated.

As soon as she had the chance, Molly would talk in private to Anna and Javi about helping the sisters learn English. Which made her think about Oliver again. He should've been part of that conversation, too. He was on her team.

And she had made the decision to abandon him.

"Mol?"

Hearing Javi's voice, Molly quickly pulled her shirtsleeve back over her shoulder. "Over here," she said.

Javi followed her voice through some desert brush and found her sitting on a rock, staring at nothing. He took a place near her, directly on the ground.

Before today, she probably wouldn't have given a second thought to how casually he had sat down. Now she did. If it had been blood sand, he'd have had to do a five-minute self-inspection to be sure the simple act of sitting wouldn't get him swallowed up.

As Oliver had been swallowed.

She clamped down on the thought, steeling herself against a wave of misery.

Javi had a stick that he used to draw in the dirt, just making circles and lines, nothing of importance. "You've got to come back to the camp."

"Not yet."

"Now, Molly. You're the leader. The team needs to see you acting confident, and looking like you know what you're doing."

"I *don't* know what I'm doing!"

"We understand that! Nobody expects you to have all the answers, or even to make the right decision all the time. But we need to see you stand up in front of us, telling us that everything is going to be okay, and that you know we're going to get out of this rift. Even if you're lying to us, say what we need to hear. Because if you can make us believe that we're getting out of here, then we'll help you make it happen. There's a lot of smart people on this team. Come and lead us."

Molly wiped at her eyes. "What would you have done back there, if it was your decision?"

Javi shrugged. "I honestly don't know. But that's why you make the big bucks. Right?"

"Yeah, sure." Molly drew in a deep breath. "All right, let's go."

The first thing Molly noticed upon arriving back in camp was Javi's shelter. He had made a sort of lean-to with the emergency blankets, the rope, and a few long branches broken off from the trees. Anna, Kira, and Akiko had dug a half-dozen deep holes near the tallest trees and Anna was trying to explain to them that groundwater should fill the holes by morning.

The sound of rustling caught their attention; something was approaching the campsite from the far end of the clearing.

Javi pulled out his knife, and Molly picked up a stick, holding it like a bat and ready to swing.

"Relax, everyone, it's just me," Yoshi said, walking into camp. "I know I'm not the one you wanted to see coming back here."

Anna gave a half smile. "Of course you are. Especially if you tell us you found food."

Yoshi's chest heaved and fell. That was his answer.

Molly lowered her stick. "No food?"

He shrugged. "I found tracks, but the *yokaze* blew them to dust before I could find the animal that made them. I'll try again in the morning."

"That's fine," Anna said. "What we really need is water. A few days without food is no big deal."

Javi made a sound in his throat that said he disagreed.

Molly crossed the camp to her backpack and pulled out two water bottles, two packaged meals from the pilot's emergency box, and what remained of the bag of candy. "Dinner is served," she said. "We'll have to divide it into seven equal parts."

"Six," Anna corrected her. "Without Oliver, it's six equal parts."

Gloom returned to the camp, and though everyone ate and drank their share, there was little conversation before they settled in for what Molly feared would be a long and sleepless night.

# 22

## Yoshi

Yoshi would never admit it aloud, but he didn't mind doing the night watch. He was sick of translating for the sisters, and even of making up creative translations when accuracy wasn't a priority. He knew Anna watched him a lot, and he had a pretty good idea why. Girls often watched him . . . until they got to know him better. Then they ran. Javi and Molly were all right, but he couldn't quite figure them out. Molly treated him the same as everyone else, like he was part of their team. What was that all about? And Javi kept trying to be his *friend*, which Yoshi especially didn't understand.

So at least when the camp settled down for the night, Yoshi could let his mind rest, too. Most of the time, he took a longer watch than the others, but he could handle it.

What he couldn't handle was having to think about facing

the group again tomorrow morning if he came back without any food. It was one thing at home to look at the disappointment on his father's face. Yoshi could shrug that off without a second thought. But he knew how hungry his teammates were. They were depending on him.

"You're my only son," his father once told him. "People will depend on you to carry on the family name with honor and pride. Why can't you respect that?"

"Because it doesn't matter," Yoshi had said. "It's just a name. Maybe I should take Mother's last name? Would you rest easy then?"

That had certainly gotten a response. Yoshi was good at pushing his father's buttons. It was slightly better than suffering the disapproving silence the man projected at all other times.

But it was different with the team. They needed him, and they made no secret of it. Somehow, that made him want to come through for them. He felt . . . responsible.

It was a new feeling for him.

He walked around the perimeter of the camp, listening for any signs of danger and watching for predators, but watching just as carefully for any signs of a cloaking device in the area, even though he wasn't exactly sure how to spot something that was by definition nearly impossible to see. Yoshi's current plan was simple: If it didn't look natural, kill it. That seemed easy enough to remember.

An hour later, everything remained just as quiet as it had when everyone first fell asleep. He was a little worried about Molly. She had a hand on the battery for warmth, but that hand was shaking, and he saw her mumble in her sleep. He couldn't hear anything she was saying, but it was probably nighttime gibberish anyway. If she kept on this way, she'd wake up even more exhausted than she'd been before falling asleep.

He reached out to touch her shoulder, just to make sure she was okay. The instant he did, she sat up, eyes wide and ready to take a swing. Hoping to avoid an inconvenient black eye, Yoshi grabbed her hand, and hissed, "It's me; it's okay. Settle down!"

She saw him, then her expression calmed. "Yoshi, I'm sorry. What's wrong?"

"You looked like you were having a bad dream."

"Oh." Molly sighed. "I guess I was."

After a moment of awkward silence, Yoshi asked, "Want to talk about it?" He figured that was the sort of thing team-mates were supposed to ask.

Molly closed her eyes. "It was just so vivid. I was back on the plane. But it wasn't exactly the same plane, I don't think, and I was—"

Yoshi shushed her.

"Really?" Molly looked offended at being cut off.

"Did you hear that?"

She gave him a skeptical look. "The *yokaze*?"

"No. Something else." Yoshi checked the flashlight tucked into the waist of his pants. "I'm going after it."

"What? In the middle of the night?"

"I'm not tired, and it's time for your watch anyway. I'll be back."

Molly got to her feet. "Your job is to protect this camp. You can't leave!"

He turned to her, feeling his temper rise. "And you can't tell me what to do."

"I'm the leader of this team. If I tell you not to go, you have to do what I say!"

"Under your leadership, almost every member of this team was nearly killed yesterday, and we lost Oliver. So you'll forgive me if I decide for myself just how I'll protect this camp."

"Don't go," Molly said. "Please, Yoshi. Our team can't take another loss."

"Maybe he wasn't lost, Molly. What if we just left him? That was your choice!"

Based on her reaction, Yoshi might as well have run her through with his sword. That was how wounded she looked. He hadn't meant it. None of what happened yesterday was Molly's fault. If he'd been the leader, he probably would have made every decision Molly had. Until now. He had heard a sound, and he wasn't going to sit around waiting for it to attack his sleeping teammates.

He pulled out his sword but looked back long enough to say, "I'm sorry for what I just said. You didn't deserve that." Then he walked out of the camp.

Both moons were high in the night sky, though *midori,* the green one, would sink over the horizon first, leaving them with an *aka*-tinted morning. He wasn't sure he was ready to subscribe to Molly's color theory, but he hoped that was a good sign. His eyes were already adjusted to the low light, so it wasn't hard to find the trail he'd been looking for.

Just as he'd suspected, the tracks were similar to those he'd seen before: big claws with a long tail that dragged on the ground. They were fresh, and Yoshi figured the creature who'd made them was nocturnal. Nocturnal, large, and nearby.

Its trail circled most of the way around the camp, leading Yoshi away from the blood sand and toward another clump of trees down a small hill. He heard rattling on either side of him, which was unnerving enough that he was tempted to go back to camp. Except he couldn't, not after the way he'd talked to Molly.

Sometimes he could be such a jerk. He knew how awful she already felt. Then he had to go and make it worse. He wouldn't blame her if she was already gathering up the rest of her team and telling them to break camp without him, to leave before he got back. That'd be exactly what he deserved.

Ahead of him, a twig snapped, and he was sure he caught the sound of a low growl carrying through the air. He gripped his sword with both hands. Whatever was out there, he hoped it tasted better than those scorpions did.

Using the light of the moons, Yoshi followed the tracks. Sand was still collapsing inward from the outer edges of the prints. The creature was only seconds ahead of him, somewhere in the brush.

Yoshi heard the growl again and stood still, keeping his sword ready for anything, and hoping the *anything* was on the scale of a large squirrel.

But he knew it wasn't.

The creature came from behind. Yoshi had started to turn, but the claw still swiped down his right arm, nearly forcing him to drop his sword. He grunted in pain and rotated his arm so the sharp edge of the sword would face the creature when he swung backward. He struck the animal's flesh but was knocked facedown before he could do any real damage.

It was some kind of large cat, like a mountain lion but with green spots that might've looked cartoonish in any place outside the rift. Here, those spots were just plain scary.

A paw came down on Yoshi's shoulder, but he rolled into the creature's weight, knocking it off balance. As soon as he freed his sword from beneath him, he struck upward. It was a good thing he did, because when the animal swiped again, claws out, it only grazed past Yoshi's arm.

Yoshi drew up his knees and kicked out, connecting with the animal, and took one more swipe with the sword. He knew he'd done some damage, but it also made the animal angrier, which was going to be a problem.

This time, Yoshi turned his sword sideways, wrapping both hands around the blunt edge of the blade and pushing it upward, just as the cat leaped on top of him. The sword protected Yoshi from the cat's sharp-toothed mouth the first time, but it reared back and prepared to come at Yoshi again.

A loud squawk sounded overhead, distracting the cat. It looked up at the sky and snarled, then turned back to Yoshi. With one swipe of the cat's paw, Yoshi's sword clattered onto the ground. He felt around for it, but it had fallen out of reach.

The cat roared at Yoshi. Its breath was warm and smelled of rot. He closed his eyes, still straining to grab his sword. Then, suddenly, the weight of the cat lifted off him.

Yoshi opened his eyes. The bird that had squawked was carrying the cat into the air. Silhouetted against *aka*, only the struggling cat and the tip of a giant wing were visible as the bird flew away.

Yoshi leaned his head back on the ground to catch his breath. As the adrenaline left him, he felt weak and tired. He was so tired, in fact, that he failed to hear the clicking sounds until it was too late.

He tried to roll away, but he was already surrounded and a stinger plunged deep into his right leg.

Suddenly, Yoshi was even more tired. As his eyes closed, he knew he was in serious trouble.

# 23

## Molly

For several minutes after Yoshi left camp, Molly had stood there, just staring in the direction he'd left. Half of her expected he would come right back, and the other half debated what to do if he didn't. She was so angry about the things he'd said that she wasn't entirely sure she wanted him back at all.

Of course she did. But he owed her a big apology.

As the minutes ticked away in her head, Molly finally had to face the fact that Yoshi wasn't returning, at least, not until he was ready to do it. Anyway, it wouldn't be a bad thing if he came back with food. Let him blow off his steam in a way that benefitted the group.

A few minutes after that, however, she heard a chilling sound in the not-distant-enough distance. It was the screech of a bird of prey—a big one.

"What was that?" Javi asked groggily.

"I don't know," she said. "But Yoshi's out there."

Together, they woke up Anna, and were only midway through their explanation before they heard Kira's worried voice. "Yoshi?"

"*Abunai*," Anna said. It was probably the wrong way to use the Japanese word for "dangerous," but it got the point across. Kira woke Akiko, and they both immediately stood, indicating their willingness to go look for Yoshi. Molly almost wished Yoshi were here to see this, how eager his teammates were to help him, even when he didn't want it.

"We should all go together," Molly said. "No more splitting up."

They started out in the direction Yoshi had gone. "Why would he risk hunting in the middle of the night?" Anna asked.

"He was . . . angry with me," Molly mumbled. "We had a bit of a fight."

"Oh, right," Anna said, as if she already knew why Yoshi might be angry. But Molly felt Yoshi's frustrations had to be about more than what had happened to Oliver. He'd been moody all day—more than usual, even.

"Yoshi." Kira had turned on her flashlight and pointed the beam at tracks in the dirt: Yoshi's sneakers. Beside them were other tracks, those of some sort of large animal. Molly didn't like that. Was Yoshi stalking the animal, or the other way around?

Kira led the way forward, followed by Javi, who was holding out his knife much the way Yoshi wielded his sword, but Molly saw his hand was shaking. She took up the rear. Nobody on her team was getting left behind this time. No one.

The trail took them around the ridge of a large mound of dirt. Leafless bushes lined their path, too small and bare too hide anything. If a predator was ahead, Molly knew in her gut that Yoshi had already found it. Or it had already found Yoshi. Her stomach knotted with worry.

Not much farther on, Kira cried out, "Yoshi!" and ran forward. The entire team followed, and by the time Molly got there, everyone else had surrounded him.

Yoshi was lying on his back, eyes closed, and with his sword just out of reach. One arm had a long claw mark from his bicep past his elbow, and a second claw mark went sideways across his shoulder, but the rest of him seemed intact. So why was he so terribly still?

"Yoshi?" Akiko whispered. Even without looking at her, Molly could tell she was crying.

Anna knelt beside Yoshi and put her head down on his chest, listening for his heartbeat. "He's alive," she said. Then she sat up and shook his uninjured shoulder. "Yoshi, wake up!"

He groaned, and his eyes fluttered, but they didn't open.

Javi kicked lightly at Yoshi's feet. "I'm going to take your sword and use it to saw wood. If you don't want me to do that, you have five seconds to tell me no."

Yoshi mumbled something, but his eyes were still closed.

"That doesn't count as a no," Javi teased. "After I use your priceless Japanese sword like a cheap metal saw, I'm going to clean it with water. Not oil, just the next batch of dirty, grimy desert water Anna finds for us. I sure hope it doesn't rust."

Yoshi mumbled again and his right eye twitched.

Anna smiled. "Once we're home, we're going to tell your father that you only took the sword from Japan because you were mad at him, and that you're not giving it back unless he lets you stay with us in America."

"Can't stay in America," Yoshi said. "Mom doesn't want me. No one wants me. Permanently."

Silence fell over the team, who all looked at Molly as if she should know what he was talking about. The only one who didn't look at her was Javi. He did know what Yoshi meant, Molly realized.

"Let's give him time to rest," Javi said. "I think he's fine."

But Yoshi wasn't finished. This time his eyes fluttered open. He looked up at the sky overhead and he said, "We were only supposed to take three sour candies, but I took four. I'm sorry. And I changed my grades on the computer when the school secretary left for the fire drill, but that was her fault because she should have figured out I was the one who pulled the alarm. And, Javi, I know you farted on the blood sand. It really smelled bad, dude."

"He's delirious," Molly said. "Probably dehydrated."

"We're all dehydrated, but none of the rest of us is talking like this," Anna said.

Javi smiled. "You always talk like this, Anna!"

She looked taken aback at first, but quickly recovered. "Hey, Yoshi, tell us your most embarrassing story. Something really crazy!"

"He's not a toy for us to mess with," Molly said. "He's just dehydrated. Help me sit him up."

But maybe it was more than that. Akiko and Kira were near Yoshi's feet, and when they sat him up, Kira said his name again and then gestured for Molly to come look at what she was seeing. She shone the flashlight on a red welt on the side of his calf with a lighter dot in the center of the welt.

"I'll bet that's a scorpion sting. Cool!" Anna quickly corrected herself. "I'm not glad to see it. It's just that we were wondering what a launch scorpion sting does. I think it's like a truth serum."

"You're pretty," Yoshi said, staring at Anna. Then his eyes drifted to Kira and Akiko. "And you're pretty, and you are." Next he looked at Javi. "And you're a dude."

"Get him to his feet," Molly said. "I'd feel better if we were back at camp for the rest of the night."

Javi wrapped one of Yoshi's arms around his neck, and Molly took the other to lift Yoshi to his feet. Yoshi's head drifted to Molly. "I've been kicked off my family's team. Why am I on yours?"

Molly stopped and made sure Yoshi was paying attention to her. "We need you on Team Killbot, Yoshi. We want you to be one of us."

He grinned like a four-year-old who'd just been given a sucker. "You're pretty, too."

"Let's go," Molly said, leading the way as they dragged Yoshi back to camp.

*Midori* was nearly finished sinking below the horizon once they arrived. Everyone was tired, yet no one was going back to sleep except for Yoshi, who needed to sleep off the effects of the scorpion poison.

Anna offered to wrap his arm and shoulder with the emergency bandages Molly had been carrying, and as she did, she said, "He probably won't remember much of this when he comes to. Do we tell him what he said?"

"No," everyone agreed. Even Kira and Akiko added in their chorus of "no," though they couldn't have known what they were agreeing to.

So when Yoshi awoke a couple of hours later, everyone was stone-faced when he asked, "How did I get back to camp?"

"We carried you here," Javi said.

"Thanks." After some long stretches, Yoshi took a seat beside Kira near their stack of wood that had yet to become a campfire. He screwed up his face as if trying to remember something. "Did we . . . talk?"

"*I* talked," Molly said. "You were delirious."

"Oh." Yoshi looked up at Molly. "I thought you told me . . . Well, I just . . . I think I need to apologize for last night."

Molly nodded back at him. As far as she was concerned, that was good enough.

Kira said something to Yoshi and he replied in Japanese, then turned to the group. "She wanted to know about last night's hunt, and I think you all should hear this." He held up his bandaged arm. "The animal that did this to me was like a cheetah. I figure it was at least eighty pounds. The truth is, it probably would've won our fight, except it was carried off by some giant bird."

Javi's eyes widened, then he grinned. "A *bird* was the predator to a *cat*?" He looked around the group. "Seriously, no one else thinks that's funny?" Seeing the rest of the team's serious expressions, he said, "Oh, wait. What kind of bird can lift an eighty-pound cat? Yeah, that is pretty bad."

"Exactly." Yoshi shrugged. "We need to start watching for materials to make a bow and arrow. My sword is a good weapon for creatures on the ground, but we need other options. Once we leave the desert behind—"

"We're not leaving it behind," Molly said firmly. "I've reconsidered. We're going back onto the blood sand. We're going to look for Oliver."

# 24

## Javi

Javi wanted to go back for Oliver, he absolutely agreed with Molly about that. But everything that came after that decision made him nervous. Such as returning to the blood sand, for example, this time with no water and less food than before. Yoshi was banged up, Molly's wound wasn't healing, and everyone was exhausted. There could be additional confrontations with those pincer robots, cloaking fields, sand grabbers, or who knew what else—he did not want to go back.

But it was for Oliver.

Javi knew if it was him who'd been carried away, when Molly proposed they go back, Oliver would've been the first to step up. Of course Javi would go.

There was just one problem.

"Molly," he said softly. "I think we need to be realistic about what we're going to find. Or not find. I think it's likely that Oliver is . . . that he's—"

"That he's alive," Molly said. "I think so, too."

"Why?" Anna said. "What makes you say that?"

"Think about it," she answered. "Someone built this place. And someone uses the mites to maintain it. And someone went to a lot of trouble to keep us alive when our plane went down. Presumably, it's all the same someone. Or someones."

"Okay," Javi said. "So . . . ?"

"So presumably the person who programmed the mites wants us alive. You heard Yoshi—they were swarming down there when Oliver was taken. I think they meant to help him."

"They didn't save Caleb," Anna said flatly.

Molly hesitated.

"Okay," Javi said. "Let's say you're right and the robots saved him. Where would they take him?"

Molly smiled, clearly grateful that he was taking her seriously. "I think our best chance of finding him is to go back to the cave where Yoshi, Anna, and Kira first saw the robots. Maybe that was, like, their mission control."

"We, uh, pretty much destroyed that cave in an avalanche," Yoshi said. "Before we can return, mission control needs a visit from the snow patrol."

"Then we have to find their new home base," Molly said. "Maybe we can pick up noises on our radio, like before. Maybe there's a trail across the blood sand that we can follow."

"Maybe not," Anna said. "It's a huge risk to take on so little evidence."

"And what about the building?" Javi asked. "That's still our best hope of finding a cure for your shoulder."

"My shoulder is fine," Molly said.

But it wasn't fine. The price for going after Oliver might be Molly's life. She had to know that.

Yoshi consulted with Akiko and Kira, then said, "If we're going to do this, we need to split up more of the food and maybe Anna could check on her water holes."

Molly agreed, and handed her backpack to Akiko to divide up the food while Anna, Yoshi, and Kira went in search of water.

"Stay with me," Molly asked Javi. He didn't know why, but the expression on her face was so tense, he knew it had to be serious.

Once the rest of the group had spread out for their tasks, Molly said, "I have a feeling we took a wrong turn on our way to that structure. I don't think we're supposed to be here at all. I want to go after Oliver to save him, of course, but I also think we need to backtrack and look for a better path through the rift."

"Where is this coming from?" Javi said. "What do you mean, you have a feeling?"

Molly looked bashful. "I . . . had a dream about it last night."

Javi shrugged. "Well, last night, I had a dream that I

showed up for school in the pink ponies shirt and tried to convince the principal that it should be our new mascot. I don't care how real that dream seemed—that shirt is gone and good riddance, and once we get home, I'm not telling anyone about it. It was only a dream, you see? So are you talking about a dream, Mol, or is it something more than that?"

He waited while Molly thought about that, and before she could answer, behind them Anna exclaimed, "Water! We have water!"

Molly and Javi joined the others in running over to her. Sure enough, in a deep hole near the tallest tree, a puddle of water had formed. It didn't look entirely hygienic, but Javi doubted anyone would care.

"We'll need to boil it first," Anna said.

"Everyone get your water bottles and fill them up," Molly said. "I'll start a fire!"

Thirty minutes later, Team Killbot had drank the last drop of their still-warm water. Anna suggested if they stayed there for the day, the hole might refill, but even she said she'd rather set out to search for Oliver. Breakfast was one large seaweed chip each, and this time everyone ate theirs. Javi even wished he could have another.

"All right, let's pack up camp," Molly said. "I want to be back on that blood sand in ten minutes."

At least with a little food and water in his stomach, the idea of crossing blood sand didn't sound as awful to Javi. Well, it still did, but he would do it, for Oliver.

*Oliver?* Javi stepped forward, almost unable to believe his own eyes.

Oliver was standing right in front of him, just past the scraggly trees at the edge of camp. He was holding one robotic sand mite in his arms, like it was a favorite puppy. The robot's long whiskers were coiled around one of Oliver's wrists, but he wasn't resisting. In fact, Oliver appeared strangely comfortable.

"Oliver!" Akiko squealed with delight and darted forward with open arms, but Javi grabbed her and pulled her back. Somthing was wrong.

He looked at Javi, but not really, and in a voice that didn't sound entirely like him, Oliver said, "You are all in danger. I am here to warn you."

# 25

## Anna

Anna had been near the back of the camp when Oliver showed up, but as soon as she saw him, she pushed past Yoshi and the sisters and ran up to Molly and Javi, who were standing beside each other, looking at Oliver with their mouths hanging open.

"What's wrong with everyone?" she asked. "Oliver!"

He tilted his head to stare back at her, but said nothing.

"Oliver?" This time, it was a question.

It shouldn't have been. Obviously, Oliver stood before them. And yet, Oliver had always stood with slightly hunched shoulders. Now his posture was perfectly straight, and he stared at Team Killbot without really seeing any of them.

"I don't understand," Anna whispered to Molly and Javi.

"Look at his eyes," Javi replied.

They were glazed over, unfocused. Distant. Like something else was using his eyes to look at them.

"Oliver, are you okay?" Molly asked cautiously.

He turned to her, and in a flat voice, said, "Molly Davis, you should not have taken the team here. We tried to stop you."

Molly looked over at Javi, her brows pinched together in concern. "We?"

"We made the river, to stop you."

"No, Oliver," Javi said. "We jumped over the river *with* you. You were there, remember?"

In return, Oliver stared blankly back at him, his forehead slightly wrinkled, looking genuinely confused.

Anna stepped forward and asked, "Who are you?"

Oliver looked at her, or through her. Then an odd smile stretched across his face, like two hooks were widening his mouth. It gave her the shivers. "You know me, Anna Klimek. I am here to help you."

Anna turned back to Molly and shook her head. This was Oliver's body and Oliver's voice, but she did not know this person. She wasn't even sure he *was* a person anymore.

"How are you trying to help us?" Javi asked. "Are you saying we should go back?"

Oliver tilted his head. "It is too late to go back. The blood sand is too dangerous. You must be careful now. You must be warned."

"Why are you all listening to him?" Yoshi asked, pulling out his sword. "This isn't Oliver!"

"Don't you dare use that on him!" Molly yelled.

"He's one of *them*," Yoshi said. "He's helping *them*."

"And maybe *they* are helping us!" This had been Anna's point all along.

Yoshi was interrupted by Kira and Akiko, and while he was translating, Molly said, "What happened to you, Oliver, after they took you away?"

Oliver shook his head. "I am good, Molly. I am fine."

"We were just about to leave, to rescue you," Javi said.

"I do not need rescue, Javi. I am safe. You are not. You need rescue."

"How?" Molly asked. "How do we need rescue?"

Oliver blinked. "We must leave the rift, before it is too late. You must help."

"Who brought down our plane?" Yoshi asked. "Do you know who did that, and why they saved us?"

"The building is good." Oliver turned back to Molly. "Good for your shoulder. *Aka* is red. Stop fighting and relax already."

The last part was an echo of Molly's own words, but coming from Oliver now, the warning sounded ominous.

"I will meet you again in the building," Oliver said. "I will wait for you there."

"Don't go!" Molly said. "Stay with us, Oliver. You're one of us."

"Team Killbot," he said, then repeated, "I will meet you again in the building." With that, he turned and walked out of camp. But it wasn't Oliver's walk. This was stiff, as if he wasn't entirely sure how to use his limbs.

Yoshi pushed past Molly to follow Oliver, and Anna went with him. The rest of the team was behind them.

"If you're going to the building, then take us with you," Yoshi said. "Let's all go together."

"Where I go, you cannot follow," Oliver said without looking behind him.

Yoshi met Anna's eyes. He looked every bit as confused as she felt.

He crossed in front of Oliver, using his body to block Oliver from leaving. "I know you're in there, kid. Talk to us."

Oliver stared back at him. His lower lip quivered. "Yoshi?"

That was him; that was Oliver's voice!

Oliver shook his head. "It doesn't . . . doesn't know how to explain—"

"What doesn't know?" Molly asked.

Whatever it was, it took control again, steering Oliver's rigid body around Yoshi and onto the blood sand.

Molly stretched out a hand. "Oliver, look at me. Put the robot down and come with us."

Oliver shook his head, though it was forced and robotic. This wasn't the bright, enthusiastic Oliver who had shaken his head on the airplane when Anna had asked him whether he'd ever flown before.

"Never in my life," he'd said excitedly.

In his life. Was this Oliver's life now?

"Do not take the bait," Oliver said. "It is *midori*. It is *abunai*. It is dangerous."

"Bait?" Javi asked. "What bait?"

"Do not do what it wants." Oliver looked directly at Javi. "It will destroy everything."

Anna crossed onto the sand, and Yoshi went with her. As soon as she put her foot down, Oliver nodded at them, then the robot in his arms dripped a spot of oil on the sand. Oliver sank down to his knees, but didn't register a hint of concern in his expression.

"No!" Molly yelled. "Oliver, let go of that—"

Before she could finish, another drop of oil fell, and Oliver disappeared beneath the sand.

"Who has water?" Yoshi said, rushing forward to the exact spot where Oliver sank. "Give it to me!"

"He's already gone!" Javi yelled.

"Then we'll follow," Anna said. "Wasn't that our plan? At least now we know he's close!"

"But in which direction?" Javi asked. "Oliver told us where to find him again. If we go to the building, that's where he'll be."

"Unless the robots are baiting us to go there," Yoshi said. "It could be a trap."

"He warned us about being baited," Javi said. "He wouldn't warn us about his own trap!"

So then, what was the bait Oliver referred to? Anna wondered. It didn't sound like he even knew the answer to that question.

But if they were going to survive the rest of their journey to the building, Anna was certain they needed to figure it out . . . or else.

# 26

## Molly

**M**olly felt the eyes of her teammates fall on her. "Options," she announced. "I want everyone's best suggestion."

"We need to go after Oliver," Yoshi said. "His trail is fresh again, but it won't last long. We have a chance to follow him."

He translated that for Kira and Akiko, who started in on their own conversation in French. Yoshi rolled his eyes, and said, "Kira and Akiko agree with me."

They probably didn't. If they were speaking in French, then they were discussing an idea they didn't want Yoshi to understand. Molly heard Oliver's name in their conversation, and recognized a few basic words, but not enough to gather anything meaningful. All she knew was that Kira and Akiko had not expressed agreement with Yoshi's opinion. They might not even know what his opinion was.

"Other suggestions?" Molly asked.

"I think we should go forward," Javi said. "Since we're off the blood sand, the devices can put us in the air again. With strong jumps, we might be only a few days away from the building, which means we're only a few days away from rescuing Oliver."

Anna shook her head. "He claimed he came here to rescue *us*. To warn us. Can we believe him?"

"Of course we believe him," Javi said. "It's Oliver!"

"Oliver's been programmed," Anna said. "Like it or not, that's the truth—you all saw that. He's a bridge between us and those robots."

"But Oliver is in there, deeper than any programming," Molly said. "We can get him back."

"Maybe," Anna said. "But we don't know that. A robot can be hooked into a computer and a new program uploaded within seconds. You can delete old programming—overwrite it, changing the robot's function forever."

"Humans aren't like that," insisted Molly.

"Aren't they?" Anna asked. "Until we know how the robots changed him—what they've done to his brain—we don't know if he can come back to us again."

"But we can't give up on him," Javi said. "I looked right in his eyes. I saw Oliver!"

"Maybe you only saw what you wanted to, because when I looked at him I saw a robot." Anna shrugged. "The question isn't only if we can bring Oliver back, it's the question of what he is now. Do you remember when we attacked the sand mites? As soon as Javi picked up one of them—"

"They all responded," Javi said. "Exactly the same way and at exactly the same time."

"What are you thinking?" Yoshi asked. "That Oliver joined their secret group text?"

"He joined their colony." Molly knew how flat her voice had sounded. She didn't want to call it that, or think of it that way, but Anna was right. The robots clearly had a shared program, so whatever happened to one of them was processed by all of them. "I'm sure he didn't want to join them, but he is one of them now, more than he's one of us."

"Exactly!" Anna said. "And we have to assume that everything Oliver knew about *us*, those robots now know."

"But all along, you've argued that those robots are good," Yoshi said. "So why is this suddenly a bad thing? Maybe if Oliver can . . . communicate with them, then that's great news for us."

"What I've said is that robots can't be good or bad," Anna explained. "It's their programmer we have to question. And whoever that is, they now potentially know everything about us that Oliver would have known—our names, our roles for Team Killbot, our unique talents, our weaknesses. Meanwhile, we don't even know *who* or *what* the programmer is."

Yoshi let out a low whistle and sat down on a rock to gather his thoughts.

"If the programmer is good, then Oliver was sent here to help us get to the building," Javi mumbled.

"And if the programmer is bad, then Oliver is a trap," Anna said. "He is the bait he warned us about."

Suddenly, Molly felt all eyes on her once again. Even Kira and Akiko were looking at her, although Yoshi had quit translating for them once they started speaking French. She remembered what Javi had said to her last night, that what the team needed most was to believe she knew what she was doing, even if she didn't.

Maybe someone else should try being the leader for a while and see how hard it was.

Finally, Molly asked, "If we knew for sure where Oliver was, how many of you would vote to try rescuing him?"

Yoshi translated, and every hand went up in the air.

"That's how I feel, too," she said. "Now, how many of you think we should still go to the building?"

Hands raised more slowly this time. Javi's went up first, which didn't surprise her. But it wasn't just about Oliver. He was constantly staring at her shoulder as if willing his eyes to develop X-ray vision so he could check on her injury, and he clearly believed the best hope for a cure was at the far end of the rift.

Kira's hand went up next and Akiko followed, then Anna.

"I think we should go toward the building," Yoshi said. "But I'm not going inside it until we know more about what we'll find there."

"I can agree with that," Molly said, and then Yoshi's hand joined the rest.

Molly crouched on the ground and grabbed a stick. Based on what Yoshi had described to her a few days ago, she drew a rough outline of the rift, put a rock at the far end to represent the structure, then drew an *X* in the approximate area where she believed them to be.

"Then we're sticking with our original goal of reaching the building," Molly said. "I think we'll find Oliver there, and we will get him back."

Hearing a question from Akiko, Yoshi asked, "The sisters want to know about the bait, what we think it is."

How could Molly possibly know the answer to that? She merely shrugged and said, "I think of what my dad used to say to me when I was a little girl: Worms don't swim. If a fish sees one, it should look for the hook." Seeing some confused expressions on her friends' faces, she added, "If it doesn't look right, then we need to be suspicious."

"That's the problem," Javi sighed. "*Nothing* looks right here."

"Better that we see it from the air, then." Molly pulled an antigravity device from her backpack. "Everyone attach yourself to a bungee cord. We're going to jump."

# Yoshi

**O**f everyone on Team Killbot, Yoshi figured he enjoyed flying—or "prolonged high jumping"—the least. It wasn't about being tied to the others, or the way weightlessness made his gut do flips. It was the loss of control he always felt in the air. On the ground, he could run or crouch or swing with his sword in a gravity he understood. In the air, he floated. Which would be great in an amusement park or as an escape from the crowds of Tokyo and New York. But in the rift, he wanted full use of his skills.

At least the desert was beginning to thin out here. There were still no visible signs of water, but Anna pointed out some grasses and small plants on the ground. If her excitement meant she expected to find water beneath the surface, he doubted there was much. The vegetation was thin and closer to brown and yellow than any shade of green. He wanted to see animal tracks, preferably another large desert cat. He didn't like the idea that he'd almost lost to one last night, and he wanted to set his record straight.

Though maybe another desert cat would bring in another giant bird to carry it away. Add that to his list of reasons why he wasn't comfortable this high up in the air. A bird like that could snatch any of his teammates in a second and be at the other end of this rift before Yoshi could even maneuver himself into fighting position. And depending on which teammate was snatched, Yoshi might just be dragged along for the ride.

If the others had seen what Yoshi saw last night, they wouldn't be enjoying themselves now. That wasn't the kind of bird anyone would want to share air space with.

But maybe they needed to have fun for a while. Javi seemed to love these high jumps, and Kira and Akiko were chattering nonstop about how much nicer it was to be up here in the air.

"Smile, Yoshi!" Kira said. "Or have you frowned for so long that your face would break?"

"It might," Yoshi said. "It's not worth the risk to find out."

After all, Oliver had enjoyed these high jumps, too.

"We might escape the desert by sundown!" Akiko said. "Can't you even be happy about that?"

He forced a corner of his mouth up when he looked over at the sisters. Was that enough of a smile to satisfy them? He hoped so, because it was the best they'd get.

"What are the others talking about?" Kira asked. "They look serious. Aren't they happy Oliver is alive?"

On the other bungee cord, Molly, Anna, and Javi were discussing theories of how Oliver might be connected to the robots, and how much control they had over him.

"If Oliver wanted to tell us something that the robots didn't want him to say, could he do it?" Javi was asking. "Or can he only say what they want?"

"What if he sincerely believes he is helping us?" Molly asked. "Maybe it's less *control* and more *manipulation*."

"If so, that's more dangerous," Anna said. "Our best chance for rescuing him is if a piece of Oliver is still fighting against them."

"They're discussing their favorite kind of ice cream," Yoshi said to Kira. That was the easiest answer to get Akiko and Kira back to their happy chatter.

"I heard Oliver's name," Kira said.

"His favorite flavor is bubble gum," Yoshi said without missing a beat.

Kira doubted him, that was obvious. And instead of going back to happy chatter, he noticed both sisters started listening more carefully to the conversation on the other bungee cord. That was fine with him. The girls didn't have the engineering background of the rest of the team, but they were brilliant in other ways. Team Killbot would benefit if the sisters could communicate with everyone equally.

"Water!" Anna shouted. "Water! We have to go down!"

Sure enough, a small pond was set amid some respectable trees and actual plants. Anywhere outside of a desert, it would be considered little more than a large puddle, but Yoshi was grateful for every drop he saw.

Once they hit land, everyone untied themselves from the bungee cords. Anna was first at the water's edge, holding out her hands in a warning against anyone touching the water. Was she kidding? They were all so dehydrated that Yoshi was beginning to feel like the prunes his American grandmother liked to eat. His tongue tasted of blood sand, which made sense. He'd probably swallowed half the desert when looking for Oliver.

"I can't find the water source," Anna said as her eyes passed around the edges of the pond. "Maybe it's a spring, somewhere below?"

"Let's boil the water," Molly said. "Just to be safe."

"I volunteer to taste it first," Javi said. "I'm the vice-deputy Spock, or whatever. I should take the risk."

Take the risk? Sure, maybe there was a risk, but Javi probably felt a lot like Yoshi did. As long as that water wasn't straight up poison, Yoshi intended to drink it.

Team Killbot moved as fast as Yoshi had ever seen, gathering up fallen sticks to start a fire, which Molly supplemented with more of the legal papers she had collected. The wood here was greener than what they'd found the night before, so it took most of the paper to start a fire, but as far as Yoshi was concerned, it was totally worth it. He'd burn his own shirt to start the fire if necessary. He wanted to get water boiling as quickly as possible.

The only reliable container for boiling was his canteen, which was now blackened on the outside from previous fires. It wouldn't offer much of a drink to each team member, but it was a start, and they could keep boiling water until everyone's plastic bottles were full again.

It was funny how much Yoshi's thinking had changed. For now, the biggest issue on his mind was his next sip of water. How silly his life was before, worrying about a high score on a video game or whether the store clerk had shorted him twenty cents on a candy bar that Yoshi would probably throw away half eaten. Yoshi wouldn't throw away a single peanut right now. He was hungry. Molly still had food in her backpack, but Yoshi wasn't sure how much, and he understood why she was saving it.

Besides, Yoshi was far more thirsty than hungry. How long would that water take to boil?

"Look at this flower!" Anna called out from a far side of the pond. "Blue petals! Molly, what do we think of the color blue? Good or bad?"

"The blue berries we ate in the jungle were safe," Molly said. "But that doesn't mean that everything blue is—"

"It's delicious," Akiko said, appearing beside Yoshi with some of the petals in her hand. "Kira and I have already been eating them. Try one."

Yoshi shook his head. "I eat meat, not flowers."

"Ask them what those taste like," Molly said to Yoshi, noticing the petals in Akiko's hands. "Are they feeling any bad effects?"

"They taste like flowers," Yoshi said.

Molly rolled her eyes and went up to Akiko. "Flower."

Akiko smiled. "*Ao.*"

"*Ao,*" Molly repeated. "Flower?"

Yoshi groaned. If they were going to teach each other their languages, they were making a terrible start.

"*Ao* means 'blue,'" he said. "Not 'flower.'"

Molly looked doubtfully at him, but he was telling the truth this time, and he really didn't care if she learned the word or not. He wanted water.

"I think it's ready," Anna said. "It's going to be hot. We should wait for the water to cool down."

"I'll try it now," Javi said, holding out his water bottle. "I don't care how hot it is."

Anna used the ends of her shirt to pick up the hot canteen and filled Javi's water bottle about a quarter of the way full. He swirled it around, letting the steam rise and commenting on how clean the water looked in comparison to the muddy liquid they'd had before.

Team Killbot gathered around him as he took his first sip. Yoshi could almost taste it in his own mouth as Javi swallowed. Javi moved his tongue around in his mouth, then smiled. "Well, I'm not dying!"

That was good enough for Yoshi. He held out a plastic

water bottle just like the rest of his teammates, and swallowed his ration even before swirling any of the steam out. It was hot and burned his throat going down, but he didn't care. He already wanted more.

"Build up the fire," Anna said. "Can anyone refill this canteen?"

Yoshi held out his hand for that job, but instead of stopping at the water's edge, he walked into the pond up to his knees, and dipped the canteen in from there.

"What are you doing?" Molly asked. "We don't know—"

"The water will be cleaner here," Yoshi said, tightening the lid and tossing it out to her. "Besides, someone had to test the pond."

She grimaced, but before she could scold him again, Yoshi closed his eyes, clasped his fingers behind his head, and fell backward. The water's welcome was cool and refreshing, washing off dirt and sand and blood. He opened his eyes, hearing a splash, and saw Kira and Akiko had joined him in the pond. Javi was next, and then Anna. Only Molly stood at the edge, staring at them all.

"Join us!" Yoshi said, standing up. He was nearly in the deepest part of the pond, and the water only came up to his chest. Even if there was some kind of predator in this water, which there didn't seem to be, he could step on it.

She was right beside his sword, where he had left it leaning against a rock, and he was sure it wasn't an accident that she stayed close to their best weapon. "I'll wait here and keep the water boiling," she said. "You all have fun."

She turned away from them and Yoshi noticed her rub her right shoulder as she did. Was that still bothering her? If so, he thought the pond water would help a lot. Maybe that was all the wound needed, a good washing.

He was interrupted by a huge splash directly in his face. He wiped his eyes in time to see Kira and Anna laughing. Not sure which of them had started it, he splashed them back, although he ended up getting Akiko just as wet. She tried to return the favor, but Javi dived between them, protecting Yoshi. "Sorry, Akiko," he said. "Dudes before damsels."

"Yoshi . . . damsel?" Akiko asked.

Javi fell into the water laughing, but Yoshi splashed him anyway. He'd successfully targeted all of his teammates now, except for Molly. But she was dividing the latest batch of boiled water among their bottles, so she'd get a pass.

By now, Yoshi doubted the water even needed to be boiled. As they splashed around, everyone had gotten some into their mouths, and they all seemed fine.

When Molly walked to the water's edge to once more refill the canteen, she came to a sudden stop, raising her hand to get their attention.

"Everyone, stop! Listen!"

When the water settled, everything went silent—except

for a buzzing sound high in the tallest tree, which leaned out directly over the pond. What was that? It wasn't a bird, or at least, not any bird he'd ever heard before. But this sound was familiar, part of a world he knew. What was it?

"Static," Kira told him. "A radio is up there!"

# 28

## Javi

Javi recognized the sound at the same time Yoshi translated the word from Kira. They already had one radio from the airplane, but it was small and cheap, and played only static. A voice was coming through this one, if barely. Maybe it had a stronger reception, or maybe it was so high in the tree that it could catch a signal that was lost at ground level. Even if the voice was faint, at least it was something. They had a chance to hear news from the outside world. Maybe they could even retrofit some of its parts to send a signal—to communicate. This was a chance for rescue!

All of Team Killbot emptied out of the pond and stood around the base of the tree, dripping wet. Javi strained his ears to catch any words through the static. It wasn't a music station—the person speaking had the serious, businesslike voice of a reporter, not the joking, musical tone of a DJ.

"Airplane," Anna whispered. "I heard the radio say 'airplane.'"

"Keep quiet and maybe we can hear more!" Yoshi hissed.

The station had gone to a commercial now. Javi could hear the jingle playing. It seemed vaguely familiar, but he couldn't quite remember the product. Some kind of fast food, he thought. Even thinking of the possibilities made his mouth water.

"We need to bring that radio down," Molly said.

"I think the reason it works is because it's up so high," Javi said. "If it comes down, it'll probably play static like ours."

"Then we'll jump up to it," Anna said.

"Shouldn't there be other signs of plane wreckage out here?" Yoshi asked. "This far from the crash site, all we have is a radio?"

"I'll bet other wreckage fell into the pond," Anna said.

Javi looked back at the water. Anything big that had fallen into the shallow water would be obvious, wouldn't it?

"I'll take the device up and see what I can hear," Molly said.

"I'm coming, too!" Anna said.

Seeing the two girls pick up their bungee cord, Kira and Akiko began tying the second cord around their waists. Javi knew they wouldn't be able to understand whatever they heard on the radio, but he also understood why they wouldn't want to be left out.

"If they're coming, I need to translate," Yoshi said, joining the girls on their bungee cord.

"We can't all sit on the branches," Javi said.

"We can keep the antigravity on and just hold on to the tree," Anna said. "Let's all go up. The volume might not go loud enough to carry all the way down here."

Javi and Anna joined Yoshi and the sisters. Molly took one device for herself so that she could sit in the branches and work directly with the radio.

With a twist on each of the devices and a coordinated team jump, Javi felt himself floating in the air. But where weightlessness had always given him a thrill, this time all he could think about was the voice on the other end of the radio, barely discernable through the thick static.

Molly had an easy time jumping into the branches, then normalized her gravity while the rest of her team merely held on to a branch near the top, keeping themselves from drifting. They were hovering above the pond, and the water rippled with the disturbance, but it was far enough below them that Javi figured it wouldn't be an issue.

And then he saw what was in the tree, and his stomach lurched in a way that had nothing to do with low gravity.

It wasn't a radio in the tree. It was a mite robot.

This mite looked much like the others, but its legs were slightly longer, more spiderlike, with sharp points that dug into the bark of the tree. It was utterly still except for a blinking red light upon its metallic body.

Javi's mind raced with the implications. And though Molly didn't ask for conjectures, the team spoke up.

"Javi, did you see anything that looked like radio equipment in the bot you dissected?" Anna asked.

"Obviously not!" he said. "I would have said so."

"Is this one way?" Yoshi asked. "Could we get a signal out?"

"Wait, wait," Molly said, and they went quiet enough to make out a few scattered words behind the growing static.

". . . emergency . . ."

". . . disaster . . ."

". . . Aero Horizon . . ."

"That was our airline!" Javi said. "They're talking about us!"

"We have to find reception," Anna said. "Before they move on to another news story!"

"How, Anna?" Javi asked. "That thing doesn't have a dial that I can see."

"No, but our antigravity devices have another setting." Molly's eyes were wary when she looked over at Javi. "We can turn up the technology."

Javi stared back at her, almost not daring to breathe. Exploding that airplane had destroyed their best chance to get home. Exploding this robot might destroy their only connection to home. This was crazy.

But it was necessary. It did them no good to listen to a broadcast that, at best, plunked out a few recognizable words here and there.

"Do it," he said.

Molly rotated her device to the correct setting and pressed

the buttons. Below them, both halves of Hercules sparked to life again and flashlights glowed on the ground, even though they were all set to off.

And a voice broke through the static. It was a man saying, "Harper, you're at Aero Horizon headquarters now. What have you learned?"

Harper, the woman who had been reporting before, answered, "There isn't much new information, unfortunately, and Aero Horizon executives are warning the families of the missing passengers not to raise their hopes with today's press conference. I'm told the only reason they are even talking now is because their last press release was so vague."

"If there are press releases, then they're still trying to figure out what happened to our plane!" Anna said.

"Shh," Yoshi said.

Harper continued, "As we're waiting for the executives to come out, let me recap what we already know. The first signs of trouble happened near Fairbanks, Alaska, though it seemed to be routine weather issues for the area. The voice footage from the cockpit didn't seem to indicate any concern by either the pilots or air traffic control."

"The plane was bumpy over Alaska," Javi said. "But that's normal, right?"

"Shh," Yoshi said.

"Two minutes later, the plane's emergency alarms went off. The pilots recorded having been hit by a bird, but this is considered unlikely. Aero Horizon Flight 16 was at twenty-eight thousand feet at the time of the strike, within the range of very few bird species, and nothing native to Alaska."

The man's voice returned. "Have Aero Horizon executives offered an alternate explanation for what brought the flight down?"

"The executives are coming out now," Harper said. "Let's see what they have to say."

Javi was sure he heard some sort of rumbling sound below them. It was low and deep. He looked at the pond water, which was rippling toward the shores, little beads of it floating above the surface. But what was causing the sound?

"Do you guys hear something?" he asked. "What is that?"

"It's just because we turned up the technology," Molly said. "Maybe the radio that we left down on the ground is echoing back with this one."

"All I want to hear is *this* radio!" Yoshi growled. "If you all would kindly shut your mouths!"

Molly's explanation made sense, but the rumble still bothered him. He was so focused on the noise that he missed the next speaker's name when he introduced himself, but he was obviously one of the executives.

"We wish to extend our sympathies to the friends and families of the more than five hundred passengers and crew aboard Flight 16," the executive said. "This tragedy has been felt worldwide, and we at Aero Horizon mourn along with you. Although our search for any signs of the missing aircraft continues, the icy waters are making that search increasingly difficult."

"They're searching the water?" Anna asked. "They won't find anything—"

"Hush!" Yoshi said.

Below Javi, the rumbling sound grew louder. It wasn't coming from their radio, as Molly suggested. Javi was sure of that now. But everyone around him was so preoccupied with the news report, nobody else even seemed to notice.

"We are doing all we can to recover the airplane's black box, which we hope will give us more information as to the cause of the crash," the executive said. "But until that time, Aero Horizon will have little more to report. As of now, all four hundred ninety-seven passengers and sixteen cabin crew from Flight 16 are presumed to be dead."

Silence followed that report, over the broadcast and among Team Killbot. Harper eventually started speaking again, but Javi barely heard her.

"They think we're all dead," Anna whispered. "That means they're not looking for us anymore."

"They're still trying to find the black box," Molly said. "Maybe they'll find us at the same time."

"Not unless we're at the bottom of the Arctic Ocean!" Anna said. "That's where they're looking."

"They're not even doing that much," Yoshi said. "Not really.

They're only telling people that to make it seem like they care about what happened to us. But they don't."

"Yoshi!" Molly said. "Of course they care."

"It hasn't even been a week yet, and they've already given up on us!" Yoshi shouted. "So let me tell you what's happening now. Their lawyers have written a carefully worded letter that's being sent to our families expressing their deepest sympathies and offering to cover our funeral expenses and maybe, if the families are really lucky, they'll get a free flight on Aero Horizon this year. Imagine the irony of that, huh? But rescuers were never looking in the right place for us. Give up any hopes you had for rescue, because it's not happening! The only way we escape this rift is if we figure it out ourselves!"

"Shh," Javi said.

Yoshi's eyes widened. "I spent that whole news broadcast trying to shut you all up, and now you're telling me to be quiet? They think we're dead—why doesn't that bother you?"

Javi raised a hand. "Just listen!"

Everyone went silent. Sure enough, the rumbling sound was growing louder. The pond water's ripples had become roiling pockets of air bubbles.

Something was rising up from the bottom of the pond.

# 29

## Yoshi

Instinctively, Yoshi looked for his sword, but he had stupidly left it on the ground before they became weightless. He'd even thought about grabbing it while he was tying himself in to the bungee cord, but he'd been so wet, he hadn't wanted to drip all over and rust it.

"Weapons?" he asked the others. "Who has a weapon up here?"

Javi shook his head. Yoshi figured he'd probably left his knife down below for the same reason. If they got through this, he had to craft a bow and arrows. They needed more weapons.

Yoshi looked down. Akiko's flute was also left behind, which would have made a decent bludgeoning tool if necessary. Grabbing a burning log to fend off any predator wasn't an option from up here. He had his fists, though, and a strong kick, and the willingness to use both if it protected his team.

Anna smacked her palm against her forehead. "The bait Oliver warned us about—this tree mite was the bait!"

Molly turned to her. "Why? To get us out of camp, away from our stuff?"

"That's not what they wanted." Javi pointed down at the pond water, which was bulging up in the center and flowing down on all sides. Something was rising up to the surface. Something very large. "They wanted us to use the antigravity. They wanted the weightlessness. Maybe the tech boost, too."

Yoshi saw it, too. It was some sort of a silvery pod, large enough that half of Team Killbot could fit inside it.

"Change the setting!" he said. "Heavy gravity. Make that thing sink again!"

"If we do, we'll all crash to the earth, too," Molly said.

Akiko grabbed Yoshi's arm. "Tell everyone we need to jump away from here. We need to leave now."

Yoshi passed the message on to Molly, who said, "All our stuff is down there. Our water, and weapons, all the food we have left, fire starters—if we leave all that behind, how do we survive?"

The pod was above the water now. Water dripped off the metal, leaving a bright sheen on the surface. The lower end of it seemed to be damaged, but the electronic lights around its perimeter suggested that whatever it was, it was fully functional. It looked like a tremendously large metal coffin—and yet Yoshi couldn't shake the feeling that something inside it was alive.

"*Akumu*," Kira whispered. Yoshi knew the word: *Nightmare*.

"Let's drift back to the ground, slowly," Molly whispered. "Nobody make any sudden movements. Gather up whatever you can in thirty seconds, then we're leaving. We'll jump as far as we can away from this thing."

She adjusted her device and pushed off of her branch. The others followed her down.

As soon as his feet touched the ground, Yoshi grabbed his sword. He looked around for his canteen, then realized Molly had left it at the water's edge.

Yoshi drew his sword.

He crept slowly down toward the pond, where the pod now drifted upon its surface.

"Yoshi!" Javi hissed. He'd followed him and now stood half a step behind him. "Let's go!"

Yoshi ignored him. He bent over for the canteen, keeping his eyes fixed on the pod.

So he didn't see what else came from the water until it was nearly too late.

A horrible, wriggling mass of green and yellow emerged from the edge of the pond, swarming over his outstretched hand. Yoshi recoiled, crashing into Javi. It appeared to be a tangled knot of snakes. Within its writhing movements he could see a score of eyes, a dozen wet red mouths. He slashed at it with his sword, but it didn't seem to make any difference. Whether it was a single organism or a whole tangled mess of them, being sliced down the middle didn't slow it down.

"Run toward us!" Molly called to them. "We need to jump!"

But in an instant he and Javi were surrounded by the slithering things, with no clear path to the rest of their team.

"Just go without us!" Javi yelled.

"Seriously?" Yoshi stared over at him. He appreciated Javi's selflessness, really he did. But when those bungee cords lifted into the air, Yoshi intended to be attached to one.

And then a loud hissing sound came from the pod.

It was the sound of air escaping.

The pod was slowly opening.

"Get ready for heavy!" Molly cried.

But Yoshi was still totally unprepared for the crushing weight that dropped him and Javi to the ground.

# 30

## Molly

Molly fell to the ground along with everyone else. Javi had fallen like a rag doll, directly over Yoshi's legs, keeping him pinned down. The slithering snakes all around them went flat. They still writhed in place, but they couldn't lift themselves from the ground. As long as Javi didn't roll over on top of them, they should be harmless.

But the pod hadn't fully sunk back into the pond as she'd hoped. It had drifted too far into the shallows. Now one end was partially submerged, but the other end was at the shoreline. Unless the creature inside it absolutely could not touch water, it was only a few steps from land. Only a few steps away from Yoshi and Javi.

"Everyone crawl to me," Molly cried. "You can do it!"

"My hands feel like hundred-pound weights," Anna said.

Despite the complaint, Anna moved forward. She wasn't quite in a crawl position—it was more like a drag across the dirt position, but she and the others were moving in the right direction. Even Javi and Yoshi had untangled themselves.

Molly stretched out to Kira, gave her the other device, then gestured for Kira to get ready. Kira rotated the dials and put her thumb near the button, waiting for Molly's signal.

Molly turned around and crawled back toward the pond.

Just as she neared Javi and Yoshi, they heard a banging sound from within the pod, like two metal hammers were trying to pound their way out.

"What is that?" Javi's eyes went wide with terror. "Mol, we have to go."

"Get to Kira. We're going to jump out of here," she told him. "But I need to do something first."

Yoshi suddenly cried out and kicked his leg back, as much as he could in the high gravity. Molly raised her head enough to see that the mass of slithering snakes had wrapped itself around one of his legs. They were coiling tighter and tighter, dragging him into the pond. He dug his fingers into the dirt, but that wasn't helping.

"I'm coming to get you!" she shouted at Yoshi. However, the banging from inside the pod was beginning to shift the lid. Whatever was inside, she couldn't let it open. She hesitated. Then, with a cry and a gurgle, Yoshi's head sank under the water. The heavy gravity would pull him to the bottom.

"I'll get him!" Javi hollered, though he was barely able to crawl himself.

"Normalize gravity for the boys," Molly shouted to Kira. When Kira stared blankly back at her, she said, "Yoshi! Javi! Up!"

As Kira began twisting the dials, Molly used a surge of strength from her infected shoulder to push herself to her feet. It was an agonizing walk toward the pod, but necessary.

"Molly!" Kira cried, then continued in Japanese.

Whatever she was saying, Molly had to make sure they were not followed. With excruciatingly slow movements, she lifted the device up and placed it atop the pod.

"How do you like heavy gravity?" she asked. Nothing was going to get that pod open now.

The banging continued as Molly dragged her feet across the sand, shuffling away from the pod. But the sounds were already growing fainter as the creature making them suffered the effects of double gravity.

She cast an eye toward the pond. Anna was on her knees in the water offering a hand to Javi, who was helping an exhausted Yoshi crawl to the shore. Kira must've succeeded in restoring their gravity.

Whatever was in the pod would not get the same favor.

Molly felt almost weightless as she crossed out of the gravity field and was sure the others felt the same way. She saw Javi was carrying something: a huge ball of snakes. Dead.

"I did it!" he exclaimed. "Me!"

Yoshi smiled. "Yep, it was all him." Then he winked at Molly, out of Javi's sight.

"Who wants dinner tonight?" Javi said.

"Anything will taste better than launch scorpions, I suppose," Molly said with a shrug and a smile.

"You're just going to leave our device behind?" Anna said.

"I don't see any other options," Molly said. And, for once, she didn't care to solicit any. "Let's get as far away from here as we can."

Nobody needed to be told twice. Kira reversed the device's gravity function, and they launched into the air, all tied to a single cord this time. They had to stay close to make it work, but they could do it. Anything to leave that pond behind them.

Molly shuddered. She thought back to a few days ago, when the mites had tried to keep them out of the desert. Was it possible they had hoped to keep her team from getting to this point, from finding that pod?

If it had opened, what would the consequences have been?

With the device's help, they floated over the desert floor. From up here, it looked so much more peaceful and quiet than she knew it was. Far behind her, the red sand stretched out like an ocean of blood. She saw giant waves rise and fall in the sand and understood what those were now.

Oliver had been left behind in the desert, yet he was still ahead of them, too . . . she hoped. She had to believe that he was, and that by the time they found him, her team would have figured out a way to bring him back. She had to trust that her team was capable of that, just as they had proven themselves capable in every other way. Whatever lay ahead, she knew they could deal with those issues, too.

The desert was slowly fading away as thick clumps of green unfolded along the horizon ahead. Not faded, graying desert green, but true green. Real trees. And with them would come water and food. It didn't have the same look as the jungle treetop, but was more forested. Molly smiled, eager to explore the forest as they drifted closer and closer to it. After the extremes of the desert, a forest sounded perfectly peaceful.

"Set us down at the tree line," she said.

When they drifted back to the ground, nothing horrible was waiting for them. The dirt was soft beneath Molly's feet. Small grasses were growing, and even a few wildflowers. Blue wildflowers that looked friendly and welcoming.

"Those have got to be a good sign, right?" Molly asked. "Maybe there's food and water ahead!"

"I dunno," Anna said. "I'm always more nervous about what we can't see."

Anna could always be relied on to say the worst possible thing. But she was right. The border of the forest was directly ahead of them, with tall, thick trees that provided a lush canopy overhead. Despite how quiet and peaceful it looked, they definitely needed to keep their guard up.

"Let's start a fire," Javi said, lifting the snakes again. "Make it a big one fit for a feast!"

"I think there's already a fire," Molly said, pointing ahead. "What's that?"

Sure enough, smoke was rising through the trees, a thin gray tendril that was carried away by the oncoming *yokaze* of evening.

"That's unusual," Javi said, obviously reluctant to continue. "What does it mean?"

It was Molly who took the first step forward. But this time, instead of the gloom and dread she had felt when crossing onto the blood sand, this step was filled with hope and even excitement. She turned around and grinned. "Listen carefully, do you know what that is?" Seeing her team's confused expressions, she said, "I hear music on the wind. Music!"

Molly had promised herself that she would save Team Killbot. And for the first time since the plane crash, she truly believed it was possible for them to succeed.

"Let's go," Molly said with a determination fiercer than she had ever felt before. The rest of her team followed, eager to see what lay ahead.

# ABOUT THE AUTHOR

**Jennifer A. Nielsen** is the celebrated author of the *New York Times* and *USA Today* bestselling Ascendance Trilogy: *The False Prince*, *The Runaway King*, and *The Shadow Throne*. She also wrote the Mark of the Thief trilogy; the stand-alone fantasy *The Scourge*; the historical thriller *A Night Divided*; and Book Six of the Infinity Ring series, *Behind Enemy Lines*. Jennifer lives in northern Utah with her husband, their three children, and a perpetually muddy dog.

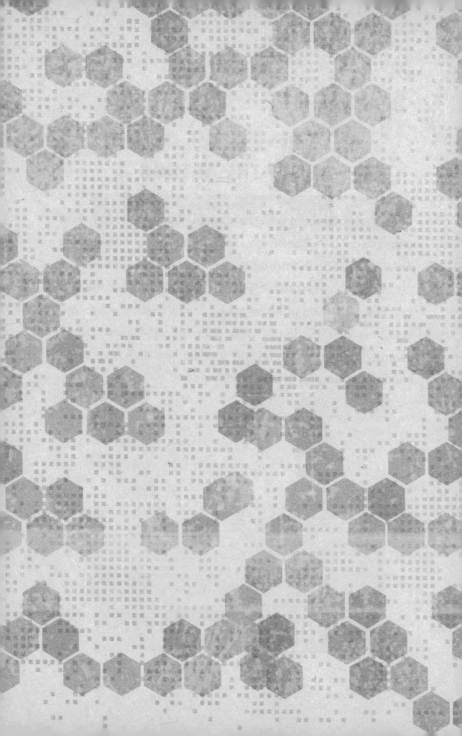

# There's even more danger
# on the horizon . . .